LIL BABY 2

SA'ID SALAAM

Urban Aesop Presents

DEDICATION

This is for the survivors...

CHAPTER ONE

"You and your damn sisters..." Big Mama sighed and shook her head. She loved these girls but they sure were a lot of work.

"I'm gonna be finer than both of them," Lil Baby proclaimed proudly, as she did every chance she got. Mainly because she idolized her sisters and the notion of one day surpassing them in anything was good news.

"Say what? Where do you get that mess from?" her grandmother laughed. Lil Baby didn't like to be laughed at so she quickly produced her proof.

"Un-huh! I heard Buck say it! I'ma be finer than both of them!" she repeated, then flew forward when her furious grandmother slammed on the brakes. Cars honked and swerved since she was in the middle of the street. Lil Baby was thoroughly confused by the outburst.

"Listen carefully gal," Big Mama said and spoke slowly and concisely. "What, exactly did you hear Buck say?"

"Nothing, they was talking about how fine Buella and Bella was but Buck said I'ma be finer than boffum!" she repeated just like Buck spoke. He said she had a fat ass already but she didn't repeat that part.

"What else you hear Buck say?" Big Mama laughed like everything was ok now. Now it was Lil Baby who changed when she lifted her chin and spoke up.

"That you kilt my daddy. That you cut his thang off and made him eat it," she repeated.

The story was a little different each time she heard it from the men but this version came straight from the horse's mouth. She never told any of the versions to her sisters since she was happy about it. Because she didn't know they suffered the same indignation as she did.

"Well, you is finna be finer than both your sisters but don't go telling them," She replied and began to drive again. Big Mama had the ability to go from zero to a hundred, then back to zero in an instant. Only sociopaths can pull that off.

"I won't," she replied, meaning she wouldn't tell them again since she had already bragged about the offhanded complement.

Had the statement been an answer on Jeopardy the question would have been, 'things a child molester would say'. For Buck to be fucking the grandmother and checking out her granddaughter snatched off an old scab that was never going to heal. Lil Baby already knew not to repeat the part about their father since she was too happy about hearing it. She had no idea her sisters had suffered the same fate as she, long before she. Or the sacrifices Buella made to save her sisters.

"Gurl what are you doing!" her grandmother reeled when Lil Baby reached over and hugged her while she drove.

"Thank you! For cutting his thang off and making him eat it!" she moaned and finally got an overdue cry for her stolen innocence and virginity. Until now the abuse had only bubbled inside and stolen her dreams. She finally got satisfaction and let it out.

"Ok gal. Get yourself together and collect our money," Big Mama announced when they reached a stop on their route. She happily watched the gleeful girl skip up to the door. Funny how vengeance makes a person happy. She put on a happy face of her own and made a call.

"Sup Big Mama?" Buck asked as he took the call.

"Look, I need you to meet me out to the house in New Iberia. Nine o'clock," she summoned. Buck began to open his mouth to reply but she had one more instruction. "And keep it yo self! Don't be gossiping!"

"OK Big Mama," he agreed since he assumed she wanted him to handle the plumbing. They met there to feed ole George, but he also laid plenty of pipe as well. They clicked off and she made another call to handle some business. "Hey..."

"Are you Ok?" Ethyl asked since after fifty years of friendship the one word was enough to tell she wasn't. By the time they hung up she had her instructions and was just as mad as her best friend.

Tonight was going to be ugly...

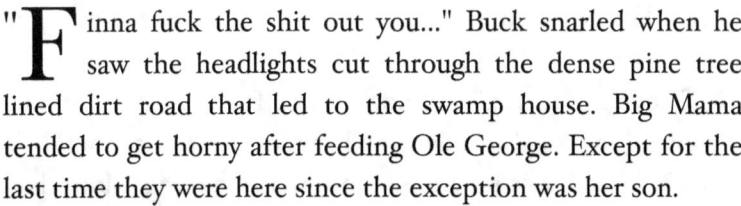

"Finna fuck the shit out you..." Buck snarled when he saw the headlights cut through the dense pine tree lined dirt road that led to the swamp house. Big Mama tended to get horny after feeding Ole George. Except for the last time they were here since the exception was her son.

"Hmp," Big Mama huffed at the smug look on her hired help's face when she pulled up. He just knew he was about to get some pussy but he was the one getting fucked tonight. She left the gun in her purse and pulled her phone. She was the only weapon she needed tonight so she got out.

"Hey there Big Mama," Buck greeted and flicked the rest of his menthol into the swamp. Big Mama flinched at the blasphemy of introducing the foreign matter to the pristine swamp but kept it to herself. He had enough to atone for at the moment.

"Hey," she sighed and headed into the house. Her eyes were drawn to the rings in the ceiling on the floor. They had trussed up many foes, a few friends and most recently family. They wouldn't be needed tonight so her eyes dropped to the floor below.

It was as clean as a place like this could be. But so much blood had been spilled below that a black stain remained. Not as black as the rust on her heart but black nonetheless. The lone bedroom was sparse, yet clean for people on the run since the house was off the grid. It was the perfect hideout with no phone or internet for people to give themselves away. Because people will go on the run but still be tethered to their social media. Then police use it to track them down and take them to jail.

Big Mama and Buck had a tryst or three in there a time or two but that's not why they were here tonight. Buck wondered exactly why as he watched her pace. She looked down at the soul-stained floor as if looking for the right words. Her head popped up as she stopped when they came to her.

"I love my family," she began. The fact that her criminal organization was also called the Family made her expound. "I love y'all, but I love my blood more than anything. More than I love myself."

"We love you too..." Buck began but was waved off by the

dainty, manicured hand. It too should have been black for all the blood it spilled over the years.

"I would die for my family. Right here, right tonight. For my family, I would," she reiterated and paused to watch his nodding head. "Would you? Die for your family? Right here, tonight?"

"For Mamie, and my 'chiren, hell yeah!" he proudly proclaimed and puffed his barrel chest even more.

"That's good to hear," she sighed, nodded, and dialed her phone. She held the device away from her ear since it was a video call.

"Hey dere!" Ethyl greeted but didn't smile. This was no laughing matter, so she reported in, "I'm here."

"Put 'em on," Big Mama ordered and went closer to Buck to share the screen with him.

"Hey there Miss Fontenot! We got the money! Thank you very much!" Mamie Johnson cheered while her extra-large grandson looked extra confused. Mamie spotted her grandson on the screen and confused him even more. "Y'all come say hey to your daddy!"

"What..." Buck began to ask but a few of his children filled the screen before he could finish.

"Hey daddy! Thank you, daddy!" Four of his youngest children sang and smiled.

"Big Mama sent money and gifts for everyone!" Mamie cheered once more.

"I..." Buck croaked but Ethyl filled the screen before he could even figure out what question to ask.

"Ten minutes?" Ethyl asked with a steely seriousness.

"Not a second more," Big Mama replied and matched her tone. The women clicked off and she turned to the confused man to explain. "You talk too much."

"Huh?" Buck asked since most people who talk too much

5

don't have a clue they talk too much. No one can tell them because they're too busy talking to listen. He was about to do it now but she waved again and continued.

"First off, you repeated what you seen here," she began and he began to stammer and stutter since lies take more effort to push out. "Don't deny it! Shit, I ain't gonna deny it! I did! I did kill my bitch ass son! So don't think I won't kill yours! And your daughters and your..."

"Fuck this!" Buck announced and turned for the door. Big Mama was unarmed and couldn't stop him.

"You ain't got enough time," she called after him and looked at the watch that was worth more than the shotgun house Ethyl sat in with his family. "Few minutes left."

"For what?" he asked.

"Before Ethyl pull her straight razor and slice your people into ribbons," she shrugged. Buck crossed the room in a chestnut blur and pinned her against the wall with her feet in the air. It certainly wasn't meant to be funny but still got a chuckle out of the woman. Big Mama looked over his retina, passed his irises, deep into his soul and laughed.

"Call her back! Tell her to leave my family alone or I'ma throw yo ass out to ole George!" he growled and pressed her against the wall with his body weight.

"told you, I'll die about mine. Right here, tonight," she shot back defiantly. He certainly could kill her, but it wouldn't save his people. Then the moon wouldn't be far enough to escape the reach of Big Mama. Even in death she could be deadly.

"What I do? So what I gossiped a lil bit!" He moaned and let her down. The gorilla tactic didn't work so he switched to a lamb and begged for mercy. "That ain't worth killing my people over! Please!"

"Naw, it ain't. But you be looking at my babies! My baby!"

she snapped on behalf of all three but Lil Baby in particular. After what she had endured his statements couldn't go unpunished. "She gonna be the finest one?"

"Nah, I meant," he began but ain't no explaining that. "I'm sorry. Please call her back!"

"No need. She finna call back in, two minutes," she replied after checking her phone. "If I don't answer, your people finna be graveyard dead!"

"What I gotta do? To make it right?" he asked as quickly as he could so as not to eat up what little time he had left.

"Jump in there with ole George," she shrugged and pulled the sliding door open. The black water below stirred to life as the sounds of the swamp filled the cabin. "If he spares you, you spared."

"I'm not finna..." Buck was saying but the phone began to ring. She turned the screen to show Ethyl's name and moved her finger to accept. "Wait!"

"No time to wait," she shrugged and accepted the call.

"What are we doing ?" Ethyl asked with a smile that belied what she would do if given the nod. Big Mama tilted her head at Buck to answer the question. She didn't flinch when he whipped out his pistol. She was ready to die about hers but that wouldn't save him. He knew it too, so he ran out the sliding down and splashed into the water below.

A young bull wasted no time and rushed towards him. He would make a nice set of boots, wallets and belts since Buck shot it right in its head. Then swam furiously for the bank. Big Mama said if he made it, he could make it and he was almost there. The few gators who swam for the free meal suddenly turned and rushed away.

"Ha!" Buck laughed triumphantly when he reached the shore.

He began to crawl out of the swamp and safety but ole

George burst from the black water and grabbed his legs. Buck turned the gun and fired but the alligator went into a death spin causing the bullets to go everywhere. Buck screamed as he was drug back into the murky water and the cold death he deserved.

"Give Miss Mamie a few extra grand to help her get by," Big Mama announced magnanimously, as if she wasn't about to have the family slaughtered.

"Come on back to the city now," Ethyl advised and clicked off. The night was still young, and they had some more killing to do.

CHAPTER TWO

"What now..." Big Mama groaned when she saw the familiar car parked in front of her house. It wasn't even a question because one thing she learned in life is that it's always something. Most beyond your control so you can only wait until they pop up. Then whack them like a game of Whack-a-mole.

"Hhn!" she chuckled at the analogy because she would love to whack the woman getting out of the car as she got out of hers. She would if she could but killing cops is bad for business.

"Hey there Eleanor!" Detective Larue cheered like her constant nemesis was an old friend. They probably could be friends in another life, had they chosen different occupations. But one was a bad girl and the other a good cop.

"How about Mrs Fontenot, since I ain't none of your buddy?" Big Mama shot back. She knew the excess venom was residue left over from the swamp. A smile contradicted the malice in her mouth, and she asked, "How can I help you?"

"Honest? Turn yourself in. Confess to trafficking in narcotics, peddling pussy, murder..." Larue laughed even though she was dead serious. She knew the woman was one of the largest players in the city but also the most elusive.

"Actually, I'm here to have a word with your granddaughter Buella?"

"I'm pretty sure them charges got dropped?" Big Mama asked even though she was sure the murder charges were dropped.

Video cameras were the new eyewitnesses and didn't make mistaken identifications. The attack and subsequent self defense was captured in stunning high definition, from so many angles it was clear. Buella was a victim who turned the tables on her attackers. That's applauded these days, as it should be.

"Yeah, not them murders. A couple more," Larue announced and shook her head. This city saw a lot of murders but this seventeen-year-old girl was attached to four already. And that's a lot, even for this city.

"I suspect you should call my lawyer then," Big Mama shrugged and turned for the house.

"If I have to arrest her. I was hoping to just get a word?" the detective offered. Big Mama pursed her lips and looked the cop up and down. Then turned her head and called for her granddaughter.

"Buella!" she said towards the house. Ethyl relayed the summons down the hall until it reached the girl's room.

"You in trouble," Lil Baby warned when she heard her tone. She spent enough time with the woman to figure out her mood by the tone of her voice.

"Prolly..." Buella sighed and rolled her eyes. They rolled over at her middle sister scrolling on her phone. She remembered how her first abortion had her feeling like the world had ended. Meanwhile Bella didn't seem to notice. She sighed again and stomped down the steps.

"Un-uh! We not doing no stomping!" Big Mama warned. "Now take yo ass back up them steps and try again!"

Buella blew her breath but did so softly since that too was an infraction. She gingerly headed back up the few steps and came back down.

"Yes ma'am?" Buella asked and didn't give the cop the respect of a glance. The slight made her grandmother proud. Her attitude towards the police was fuck the police.

"Dis cop here got a question for you..." she said, and they both turned to the detective.

"About your friend, Sadie McMillan," Larue put out and registered the reaction to the name. There was no answer, so she continued. "I'm sorry for your loss. You didn't see the shooter?"

"Naw, cuz I was too busy making sure me and my sister ain't get shot!" she shot back. A few months ago she would have looked to her grandmother for support and confirmation but she had grown a lot since then. Hardened a lot since then.

"Yeah," Larue nodded since she saw that part on surveillance footage. Including the part where she looked directly at the shooter just before Sadie jumped in front of him. "Who was y'all beefing with? Was this about y'all heroin sales? You step on some toes?"

"Heroin? Chile you barking up the wrong tree nah!" Big Mama laughed. She laughed a little less when she glanced at Buella but wouldn't let up. "This girl finna graduate. Top of her class! I'm throwing her a nice shindig. You come on out, you hear..."

"Mmhm," the cop nodded at the tacit victory. Then went in for seconds. "Why did Sadie kill Bryant Chapman?"

"Who!" both Fontenot females shot back. Buella had

actually known the first name but didn't connect it with the last name. Nor did she have any idea she had murdered the man, let alone why she would. The last she saw him; he was digging Sadie out really well.

"Bryant Chapman..." she repeated and produced the picture of him alive and smiling. She had another picture of him stretched out at the morgue but kept it in the folder.

"I ain't know he was dead?" Buella reeled with a realism that can't be faked. The older woman shared a glance and semi nod since they both believed her.

"Well, I hope that answers yo questions..." Big Mama said and gave her granddaughter a nod. Buella obviously understood since she turned and headed back up the stairs and into the house.

"Shit!" Lil Baby fussed when her sister almost caught her eavesdropping. She ran back to the room and posed on her bed.

"I don't like you one bit," detective Larue offered matter factly once they were alone again. "Hate, it's probably closer to hate..."

"I'm sure I'll sleep just fine even with that revelation," she laughed.

"But that gal is getting in over her head. Heroin, murders..." she sighed and trailed off. She watched the movie theater shooting enough times to know the shooter was shooting at Buella. Sadie just took the bullets that were meant for her anyway.

"And I said she gone be fine!" Big Mama reiterated and stomped up the steps herself. She slammed the door behind her and called. "Buella!"

"Yes ma'am?" Buella replied as she rushed up the hallway. Lil Baby hopped up and trailed behind to make sure she didn't miss anything. Bella just kept on strolling since she was only concerned with what concerned her.

"What the hell is that woman talking about?" Big Mama demanded.

"My friend was slinging, but Ion got nuffin to do with that!" she vowed. She saw the woman might buy it, so she brought it home. "Why would I do that when you give us so much?"

"Mmhm, yeah," Big Mama hummed as she chewed on the answer. Her head began to nod when she swallowed it hook, line, and sinker. "Go on, get some rest."

"Night Big Mama," Buella sang and hugged her neck before skipping down the hall. Ethyl twisted her lips but kept them pressed together. Love can blind and even though she loved the girls she still saw through that bull shit.

"You a wild boy!" Claude said, shaking his head. The shooting was a top story on the news as well as the street. The streets have their own CNN, as in country nigga network and news travels at the speed of social media.

"Told you I was gone get that goofy hoe," Wayne laughed even though he only got one. It obviously got his point across since Nick just called him for a re-up. Putting Sadie in the morgue put her out of business. After all it was strictly business, so he got down to the business of selling heroin.

"What that bag talmbout?" Claude asked on behalf of an internal itch. His arms weren't quite long enough to scratch it but a bump of boy up his nostrils would definitely soothe it.

"Spend a dime and find out..." Wayne replied and tossed him one of his ten-dollar sacks. Claude wasted no time and bit the tip off the bag. He dumped some of the skag on the back of his hand and snorted it.

"Mph," he winced when the bitter powder leaked into the back of his throat. He closed his eyes and leaned back for the rush of euphoria that was to come. Or was supposed to come but he only got a trickle. The itch was scratched but nothing much beyond that. "Eh..."

"Ten bucks!" Wayne laughed. He didn't give a fuck about how high his customers got. His pockets were all that mattered which was how Sadie was able to knock him out the box so easily. Her better bag sold better so he did the next best thing and killed his competition.

"Yeah," Claude agreed and gave him thirty dollars since it was going to take two more for him to actually get high.

"Check," Wayne said and made the sale. He grabbed the same gun he used to murder Sadie and tucked it into his waistband. He began his rounds until he wound up in Nick's ninth ward shoot house.

"Maaaannnn," Nick groaned and twisted his lips as he let Wayne into the house. He hated going backwards to the stepped-on dope but Sadie was down at the morgue so he had no choice. He wasn't heavy enough to shop with Pierre just yet, so it was best he stay in his lane.

"Want me to go?" Wayne dared and pretended to turn away. Nick didn't want him to leave but wasn't going to ask him to stay either. He shrugged his shoulders and headed into the kitchen. The creaky wooden floors told him the man was on his heels, so he retrieved his money.

"Pssssh," Nick hissed and twisted his lips as he handed it over.

"See what you talking about here..." Wayne said as he counted the money. It reached what it was supposed to reach so he reached into his bag and came out with the dope.

"Maaannn," he groaned again and twisted his lips again at the discolored dope. It had so much cut in it that what was nearly white when it started off was now an ugly gray.

"You ain't finna shoot it my nigga!" Wayne snapped in defense of his product. He knew Wayne wasn't a user and didn't understand customer service. "Why the fuck you care how high a junky get? Fuck them junkies!"

"Nah, just finna lose money," he sighed. It was exaggerated since he wouldn't exactly lose. In fact, the junkies would have to spend more to get high but word of mouth is everything in every business. Once word got out about the killer bag the junkies were beating down his door. Now once word spreads of the mediocre bag it would definitely slow.

"Whatever..." Wayne laughed and stepped back into the night.

～

"Well..." Ethyl began and sighed to soften the news. "Chile," Big Mama sighed as well. She sent the woman for answers and knew it wasn't going to be good. "Let me hear it."

"Her lil girlfriend had a nice lil hustle going. Moved up to shopping with Pierre," she reported. "And guess what pretty, yellow girl just happened to be with her when she did?"

"So, is she just tagging along? Or is she dealing?" Big Mama needed to distinguish.

"Not sure. Guess we finna see," Ethyl reported.

"Now to the good part. Who was shooting at my babies?" she asked with a glee more fitting for weddings than funerals.

"Remember Big Wayne? Used to hold down Calico back in the day?" Ethyl asked with a glimmer in her eyes.

"Ole pretty, big dicked, black muthafucka! I 'member him," Big Mama cheered affectionately for the man. Her face changed a moment later with a revelation. "I know he not still slinging from the graveyard?"

"Naw, but his son shole following in his footsteps," her right-hand woman reported.

"Well, you know where them steps finna lead him," Big Mama shrugged. And with that movement of her shoulders the man was as good as dead. "Who we got?"

"Juice got the men," Ethyl replied and twisted her lips. The man had been running the men for years until Big Mama promoted Buck.

"Yeah," she sighed as an admission of guilt since she had thought with her vagina just like men thought with their dicks. "Have him reunite father and son."

"Done," Ethyl said and stood. The patter of footsteps scurrying away didn't surprise either of them since they both knew who was listening from the hall.

"May as well send her with him," Big Mama laughed. She was training the child to take over her operations one day so she would have to see that part of the game as well.

"Hmp," her friend huffed and stepped out of the house. "Say, Juice?"

"Ma'am?" he replied and stepped over.

"You know that boy called Wayne? Daddy was from Calico," she asked.

"I remember Big Wayne. Can't rightly say I know his boy?" he replied and looked over to his men. He was sure one of them would or could, so he continued. "What about him?"

"Boss wants him to meet his daddy. He the one took shots at Buella," she reported and sealed his fate.

"Say less," he said, since she said enough.

"Sup boss man?" Trip asked when he came back over.

16

"Word came back on the shooter. Lil nigga called Wayne." Juice relayed.

"Ninth ward Wayne?" Chad asked with a murderous twinkle in his eye. The mess he made of Dame and Buford earned him some points and he was eager to earn some more. Plus, he enjoyed what he did.

"That's the one," Juice nodded and gave the nod to the dealer.

"Say less..." Chad said, accepting the task.

CHAPTER THREE

"Awe man," Buella pouted when she pushed the door open to Sadie's apartment. Her lip quivered, trying not to cry but the battle was short and she lost.

She felt the warm tears streaming down her face but didn't bother to knock them away. They were valid and appropriate, so she let them flow. Even if they did slow to a trickle when she looked into the bedroom.

The memory of the sights and sounds of Bryant delivering the dick came rushing back to her mind. She heard the head-board tapping the wall with each squishy, squelchy stroke. She recalled the way his ass cheeks clenched when he dug deep and the moans that came with it.

"Shit!" Buella reeled when she realized she was actually getting turned on. The throbbing in her panties shook her out of the spell and she remembered why she was here.

She had stolen her and Sadie's bomb as payback for the back shots she walked in on. Hiding it in the room she shared with her sisters was proving difficult since Lil Baby was nosey and didn't understand boundaries. The last thing she needed was her stumbling across the bomb of raw heroin.

A shiver ran up her spine at the thought of her baby sister getting a hold of the poison. Which reminded her of the growing itch that needed to be scratched. She pulled out the bomb with the intention of scratching that itch until a warning rang in her mind.

'Put you at least a five on that thang 'fo you turn it loose,' came to mind in Pierre's voice. Followed by the warning of his doorman, *'Anything less, they gonna be dropping like flies,'*

"Probably should put a six on it then," she reasoned out loud. That was Sadie's plan anyway once they got the reputation for the bomb bag. It could still take another step and be a step ahead of the heavily stepped on dope on the streets.

Especially since Wayne added two more steps as punishment for his customers jumping ship. He was making more money from the inferior product, and no one dared challenge his business again after putting Sadie in the dirt.

"Ok, we got this..." Buella said out loud as she broke out all the ingredients to mix the dope. She added the right amount of uncut dope to the grinder and hit the switch. Her body began to tingle in anticipation of opening the lid.

She was as giddy as a child on Christmas morning when it was time to tear into the wrappings. The moment arrived when the powder was broken down sufficiently. She smiled at the puff of dust that floated up when she opened the lid.

"Mm-mm," Buella hummed and inhaled the dust from the air.

The effect was instant and buckled her knees. She sank to the kitchen floor and leaned against the counter to nod. Buella pulled out of the nod after a while and stood. She twisted her lips at the heroin in the grinder for a moment, then got to work. The sucrose was disguised as regular sugar so she pulled it out and began to mix.

The packaging was where she and Sadie kept it, so she pulled it out and began to bag and pack. An hour later she was looking at thousands of dollars worth of work. Her lips twisted to the other side of her face as she thought about what to do with it.

"Hmp!" she huffed at the notion of being scared of Wayne. She didn't even flinch when he pointed his gun in her face. She only moved to cover her sister. She moved now to see if Sadie's other gun was where she left it. It was along with the money she left behind.

"Dang!" Buella reeled when she came across the neat bundles of cash. A flick through a stack added up to two thousand dollars and there were twenty of them.

Buella blinked and processed until she came to a conclusion. Sometimes the best thing to do is nothing so she put everything back where she found it. Then added the dope she just mixed, minus a few bags for herself.

◇

"Hey," Bella sang and nervously looked down at Chad's feet.

"Hey, ya self," he replied and looked over at the house to make sure Big Mama wasn't watching. It didn't take rocket science to figure out what happened to Buck so no one wanted to try their luck.

"She went to the store with my sister," Bella answered his look at the house. "Thank you. I heard what you did."

"I ain't do nothing," he shrugged and changed the subject. "What grade you in?"

"Finna be twelfth," Bella sighed. The school year was finally ending but what a school year it had been. "You?"

"Me? I graduated," Chad asked and answered. He didn't cross a stage or get a certificate, but he had definitely graduated. With a houseful of siblings and next to nothing parents he was the head of the household.

Big Mama's family paid better than the fast-food joints and factory jobs his education level left him at. Like many men in the hood, he wanted more than he was willing to work for so he got it how he lived. His reputation as a shooter got him recruited to the winning team during a recent turf war.

The Family won this one, but it wouldn't be the last one. There was just too much money involved to not fight for the crown. It would remain on Big Mama's head until someone was man or woman enough to take it. Even if it meant her head was still in it.

"When you gonna ask me out?" Bella abruptly asked and caught him off guard.

"Huh? Who? Um..." he stammered.

"Yeah, you. I be seeing how you be looking at me," she teased and enjoyed watching him squirm.

"Nah cuz, I be, shoot..." he stammered some more while she took his phone from his hand. He watched as she tapped her phone number in, then posed for a selfie for the contact.

"Hit me..." she said and walked back towards the house.

"I'ma hit you alright," Chad nodded as he watched her round ass shift from side to side until she was inside. He inhaled, exhaled, and turned for his car. The night was young, and he had work to be done.

"Careful..." Trip warned when Chad came back smiling.

"I'm is," he laughed since he didn't go inside any chick raw. "Wayne need to be careful."

"Too late for him," Trip shrugged since his book of life

had reached the last page. They had junkies on payroll watching for any sighting of the marked man and he had finally been spotted. "The call came."

"Let's ride then!" Chad cheered and selected a weapon for the night. Juice had just secured a load of H&K automatic machine guns, and this was the perfect chance to try them out.

"Shit, why not!" Trip agreed and grabbed one for himself. They were on reserve for the next war, but Juice gave the nod. "You driving."

"Ok," Chad sighed since he preferred to ride shotgun since he was a shooter. They rode over a few blocks to collect another car for the task. The dark sedan with darkened windows was perfect to do drive-by shooting.

"I should fuck that ole pretty bitch now that ole girl in the dirt," Wayne reflected. He was thinking about still killing Buella but couldn't shake how pretty she was when he aimed at her.

"You kilt her girl right in front her face and you think she finna fuck with you woadie?" Claude exclaimed to make him hear how ludicrous it sounded.

"Shit, the bitch like money and I'm getting money!" Wayne cheered and flipped through the stacks of cash he just made from making his rounds around town.

"You expecting somebody?" Claude asked when the headlights illuminated the front window as a car pulled into the driveway.

"Naw..." he replied and pulled his pistol. Wayne wasn't smart enough to throw away dirty guns and this one had quite a few bodies on it already. He walked over to the door to add a few more if he didn't like what he saw. He didn't like it at all when he saw Trip and Chad jump out with the machine guns.

"Ok then!" Trip cheered when he saw their target appear.

"Aaaaah!" Wayne shouted as he tugged on the trigger. The large revolver sparked in the night and lit up his face. Both shooters let theirs go as well.

"Mmph..." Trip grunted when one of Wayne's rounds slammed into his chest and sent him back peddling. Chad pressed forward spraying bullets. One of his rounds caught Wayne's leg as he turned to go back inside.

"Shit!" Wayne grunted when the slugs tore into his calf. Claude pulled his own gun and aimed at the door. Then opened fire when Chad burst in firing wildly. They both caught each other in the torso but only one was wearing a vest.

"Argh," Chad grunted when the slugs slammed into his vest and sent him right back through the door. Claude didn't make a sound since Chad's rounds came out his back and slammed into the wall. He dropped and stared off into the afterlife as his soul leaked from the bullet holes.

Wayne reloaded and flipped the coffee table over as cover. He probably should have spent more money for a better table because Chad sent a volley of automatic gun fire that tore through the pressed particle board like it was paper.

"Ok! Ok!" Wayne surrendered when several more rounds found their mark. He had lost the gun fight, so he switched to diplomacy. He tossed the pistol over the table and raised his hands. "I got money woadie. Give me a pass!"

"Where?" Chad demanded as he inched closer with the laser site on the middle of his head.

"Right chere..." Wayne pointed with his head.

He watched as Chad's eyes shifted to where he pointed and tried his luck. Chad glanced over at the money but saw when Wayne went for a second gun. He quickly tugged on the trigger and put his innermost thoughts onto the wall behind him.

"Appreciate it woadie," Chad said of the nice tip laid out on the counter. He scooped up the cash but left the drugs behind for the cops to steal. Word was out that it was trash anyway, so he rushed out to check on his partner.

"You got 'em?" Trip grunted and pressed his hand to the hole in his midsection.

"I got him," he assured and helped him into the backseat. "You good?"

"Naw nigga! I'm shot!" Juice groaned. "Take me to the hospital!"

"I got you!" Chad agreed but he knew the rules. Hospitals have to report gunshot wounds and these gunshot wounds were tied to a double homicide. He pulled his phone and made a call instead.

"Is it done?" Juice asked when he took the call.

"Yeah, but bruh got hit," he reported as he drove with no destination in mind.

"How bad?" Juice asked since it mattered. Chad glanced into the back seat and was met with a moan.

"Bad..." he replied with a heavy sigh.

"Meet me on Bourbon," came the reply.

"Ten minutes," Chad replied and changed directions. Ten minutes later he spotted Juice who pulled out to be followed. The city passed by the windows until they were no longer in the city.

"Bruh, I need a doctor," Trip pleaded from the back seat. "I'm getting cold woadie."

"I got you," Chad replied and looked at the signs heading for New Iberia.

He had heard something about a swamp from Buck but had never been out here before. This was reserved for the inner circle, so he just received a promotion. In a twist of hood irony, he was replacing the man bleeding in the backseat who had been out there before. Some time later they turned in the middle of some trees and headed down the dirt road that led to a house.

"Where are we..." Trip asked with worry in his tone. The sounds of the swamp were confirmed by the smell of the damp air. "Un-uh! I'm ok! It's not that bad!"

"Yeah," Chad sighed as he parked behind Juice. He had no idea who lived here so he didn't understand the panic in the man's tone. "This a doctor?"

"Huh?" Juice asked in confusion. He had no idea Trip had been moaning for a doctor the whole ride out. "Bring him..."

"Naw woadie. We ain't gotta do this! I'm good!" Trip assured as Chad pulled him from the backseat. He proved it by pulling away and standing on his own two feet. "See!"

"I see," Chad said when the man fell on his face. He scooped him up and carried him into the open door. His eyes automatically pulled to the open sliding glass door that led nowhere. The blackness of the swamp was all to be seen.

"Over here," Juice called and beckoned him over. They were both relieved to see Trip's eyes closed in hopes he passed away. The shallow breaths proved he only passed out before Chad laid him in front of the door.

Juice crossed his heart and rolled the sleeping man into the water. The gentle splash was met by furious splashing as the younger gators fought for the free meal. Three grabbed limbs and went into a death roll that removed both legs and an arm.

"Yeeeooow!" what was left of Trip howled. The scream was short lived when he was pulled under the murky water. Ole George missed out on this meal since the younger gators got to him first.

He was getting slow in his old age, and it was just a matter of time before some young bull claimed his spot.

Meanwhile Juice watched as Chad blinked in disbelief at what he just witnessed. His hand instinctively reached the spot where the bullets had flattened against his vest. Then his eyes rolled over to Juice looking back.

They had a tacit conversation that affirmed it could be either of them next in the swamp. It wasn't personal at all. Strictly business and this was the cost of doing business. They nodded in the mutual understanding and moved on to the next issue.

"What about the car?" Chad asked. It had bullets that would link back to the double homicide as well as blood from a third body that would never be found.

"Marquis will come to get it," he replied. The man owned a junkyard and could do to a car what Ole George could do to a body.

CHAPTER FOUR

"Y'all girls get ready to go," Big Mama ordered as she stuck her head into the girl's room.

"Yay!" Lil Baby cheered since she was ready to get out of the house. The room always seemed smaller on the weekends when both sisters were home. Both had recently lost their lovers and moped around the house.

"Where we going," Buella moaned but it wasn't a question.

"I don't even care!" Bella gushed and scrambled to get dressed. She was done mourning and recovered from the abortion. She and Chad spoke, flirted and plotted but still hadn't gotten the opportunity to hang out.

The girls readied themselves and met their grandmother in the living room. Big Mama snickered as checked each over and took in their similarities and differences. All shared the same pretty features donated by their pretty mother. Their father was just as handsome as he was perverted so he added to their good looks as well.

Growing up in such close proximity to each other didn't

diminish their individual individuality. Buella dressed like a stylish tomboy in name brand sweats and sneakers. Her long hair was kept in big braids that ran down the back of her head and halfway down her back.

Bella was a sex pot who favored short skirts and tight shirts. Today she rocked knee socks and a mid thigh plaid skirt that gave Catholic school vibes. A tight, white, button-down shirt threatened to bust at the buttons and put her breast on display. Her luscious locks were always kept in curls and swoops that gave haters something to hate.

Lil Baby fell somewhere in the middle of both sisters. She preferred pants to dresses and skirts, but her growing breast needed to be seen so she wore tight shirts like Bella. Poca-hontas braids fell from each side of her head, but she kept a New York Yankees cap on wherever she went.

"Where we going?" Lil Baby demanded as they stepped from the house.

"To see a man about a mule!" both Buella and Bella replied before their grandmother could.

"Pretty much!" Big Mama agreed. She glanced over to where Bella was cheesing and saw Chad cheesing back. She pursed her lips in thought to see what she thought about it. The fact that he slid into the car beside Juice got him a point since he must trust him to have him riding along with him. She trusted Juice with her security so he would trail her wher-ever she went.

"Un-uh lil girl," Buella checked when Lil Baby attempted to take the front seat with Big Mama.

"Uh, I always ride up front!" She checked right back and turned to their grandmother for confirmation.

"When she not here," came the clarity. There was a pecking order amongst siblings and Big Mama respected it. Lil Baby had been popped enough about sucking her teeth, so she just twisted her lips and climbed into the backseat with Bella.

"Can we get some oyster Po boys?" Bella wanted to know since she was hungry almost as much as she was horny.

"Eww, I want crawdads!" Lil Baby tossed in her request.

"I could eat," Buella cosigned since she was pretty hungry. The heroin made her neglect meals, and it was going to start to show.

"We can eat," Big Mama agreed. Then basked in the musical banter of three teenaged girls in the car. No one even noticed when she pulled in to see the man about the mule.

"What's this place?" Buella asked hopefully. She turned to her grinning grandmother, but the answer came from the back seat.

"Uh, the sign says BMW..." Lil Baby replied and rolled her eyes.

"Ooh I want a BMW!" Bella cheered and bounced.

"Next year when you finna graduate," Big Mama replied and confirmed why they were here. She had been promising to buy Buella a vehicle and the time arrived with graduation weeks away.

"That's it!" Buella said and pointed at an all-white X-5. It was a few years newer than the all-black X-5 Sadie used to drive but she didn't know the difference.

"Hey there ladies..." a handsome, black salesman greeted and grinned as he made his way over. His eyes shot all over, up and down the girls before he asked. "What can I help you with today?"

"By getting Tony," Big Mama snarled. She didn't like the way men looked at the girls, especially Lil Baby who had filled out by the day. She didn't have to poke her chest out anymore once her breasts rounded and plumped. She still had the mind of a girl which made her vulnerable.

"T,t,Tony?" the man stuttered like he was confused. He usually handled most of the black clients who shopped with the dealership.

"Y,y,yes. You know, the owner..." she shot back. Her girls heard her tone and came closer. If something popped off, they were close enough to do some of the popping.

"Mrs Fontenot!" Tony boomed when he rushed from the office. The black salesman still looked confused, so he clarified with a, "Fuck outa here!"

"Can't shake that New Yawk accent I see!" Big Mama laughed and allowed the man to hug her. Buella and Bella looked at each other for explanation but replied with shrugs.

Lil Baby knew who the man was since she made rounds and eavesdropped on enough conversations to know most of the Family business. She could probably run day to day operations herself if something happened to Big Mama. Which was exactly what Big Mama wanted since something happening to her was inevitable.

"What can I get you guys?" he asked and cast respectful glances at the girls. "Let me guess, convertibles?"

"Yes please!" Bella gushed since she had been eying a red 3 series with the top down since they pulled in.

"Next year on the drop top," she replied to Bella, then turned back to the owner. "My baby wants that X-5,"

"Bobby, grab the keys for the white X-5!" Tony called over to the salty salesman. He disliked being a gofer but not as much as he disliked being unemployed so he rushed to grab the keys. Big Mama watched his eyes again to make sure they didn't roll over her girls.

"Here you go. Want me to write it up?" he said in hopes of commission since the owner didn't make sales.

"Nah, I got it," Tony replied and passed the keys to

32

Buella. She stood there smiling and bouncing like she didn't know what to do.

"Well, take it for a spin. Try it on for size..." Big Mama was saying but the girls were already climbing in. Usually, a salesman accompanies a buyer, but these weren't ordinary buyers. Tony said nothing as the vehicle pulled from the lot.

"This put us about even?" he asked and scrunched his face like he was calculating.

"Not even!" Big Mama laughed and cracked them both up. "I think the red convertible might set us about right..."

"A little lopsided your way but we'll catch it up on the next run," he nodded in agreement. He was making great money off the heroin she supplied and didn't mind the bartering system.

"Just hold on to the car for a couple months. That goofy gal ain't ready to be riding around on her own yet," Big Mama decided. Buella would be leaving for college after the summer so Bella would have to grow up real quick.

"Want me to put something aside for the other one!" Tony exclaimed eagerly.

"For the little one?" Big Mama laughed. "Trust me, she coming to get her own car before we know it!"

∽

"Let me go with you?" Lil Baby asked when Buella prepared to leave. She missed hanging out with her sister but was also on a mission since she heard Big Mama and Ethyl speculating about the girl. They were wondering what the girl was up to so she would find out and report back.

Ethyl swore she was on dope, but their grandmother insisted on everything else under the sun. The girl hid her fledgling drug habit as best she could but still couldn't get by the eye of an ex-junkie herself. Ethyl casually used heroin for a decade without it getting the best of her. It still got some of her before she managed to shake it off for good. People married heroin for better or worse.

Big Mama saw the signs as well but wrote it off to grief since the girl's girlfriend just died. That's why she bought the graduation prize a few months earlier. It seemed to work since she wasn't moping around anymore.

"Naw," she shot back and continued to get dressed. The small monkey on her back was beginning to stir and wanted some attention. Plus, she had a funeral to attend.

"Hmp!" Her sister huffed and pointed at her with her fingers like Miss Ceily did Mister before leaving with Suge. Buella flinched when it seemed like the girl could see straight through her.

"Mmhm," Big Mama hummed when Buella walked through the house and out the door. Bella and Chad were huddled up close but stepped back when the front door opened.

"Where you going?" Bella asked but was just being nosey since she didn't want to go. She wanted to go somewhere with Chad, but he was on the clock.

"To mind my business," she said over her shoulder and pressed the key fob. Her eyes lit up along with the lights on the truck. The new vehicle didn't make the grim task any better, but it still had to be done.

Buella pumped the radio but didn't hear much of what was said. She didn't miss much since some rapper was rapping about the same foolishness that caused the funeral she was heading to. The devil used the devilish music to indoctrinate legions of youths to evil behavior. The small church was lined with cars as family and friends came to pay their respects.

"Huh?" she asked no one when she saw what looked like

Sadie's truck. She parked behind it and headed inside. All heads turned to see who came in even though the preacher was steady preaching. It was pretty much like the rapper who was rapping on the radio since he wasn't practicing what he was preaching either.

Buella slid into a pew and looked at everything and everyone instead of the pretty girl laying in the box. She focused on the large picture standing beside the casket of Sadie in better days. Even her worst day was better than the day she died.

"Hey..." Nick whispered as he slid in next to Buella. "I needs to holla at you."

"Hey?" she asked, wondering why he was talking while the preacher was talking. Then noticed the preacher was done preaching and people were lined up for a final word before they closed the lid.

"I'll be here..." he said as she stood to join the line of well wishers. Nick locked onto her ass and traced her panty line through her sweatpants.

Buella had time to gather her thoughts as the line crept forward. Sadie was loved in life and would be missed in death according to the final sentiments of those who had their say. She still hadn't found the words before she found herself looking down at her dead friend.

A shiver shot through Buella's soul when she realized it could very well have been her stretched out in the box. Would have been had Sadie not stepped up and taken those bullets for her. The man who killed her was in the back, waiting on his turn to be mourned even if he wouldn't be missed.

"Thank you," Buella said at her friend. Words bubbled in her brain, but none made it to her mouth. She touched her cold hand and turned to leave. Nick was true to his word and waited near the door. "Hey?"

"Shit, I need to mess with you. You still working?" he asked and noticed her stumble away. "You good?"

"Uh, yeah," she recovered when she remembered Wayne was next up in the church. She watched as Sadie's mother got into the vehicle she inherited from her daughter. She let out a sigh of relief that no one knew where the apartment was. That meant the money and dope was safe which also meant she was back in business. "Hell yeah!"

"Double me up!" Nick cheered and pulled a wad of cash from his pocket.

"Hole up!" she laughed and pulled back. Even the smell of money turned heads in the hood. "I'll fall through in a few..."

CHAPTER FIVE

B uella felt like a boss when she reached the apartment. She made a few calls to fill the void left by Wayne's passing. Everyone was willing and ready to shop with her again after the bullshit bag Wayne forced on them. She loaded up and headed for the door then a thought spun her back around.

"I ain't going out bad," she announced to no one as she collected the gun. She tucked it into the waistband of her sweatpants, but it quickly fell down her leg and out the bottom. "Hmmm?"

Buella was never a purse girl since she never had much to carry in one. She did now so she selected one of Sadie's designer bags from the closet. She didn't know enough about fashion to know a knockoff from an original but didn't care. She tucked the gun inside and headed back into the night.

"I'm on the way. Be there in a few. I can't drive no faster!" Buella replied to all callers as she made her rounds. Each stop left her with less drugs and more cash. She barely had enough to fill Nick's order since she saved him for last.

"Where the hell you been!" Nick demanded as he pulled her inside. Buella fixed her mouth to fuss but the sight inside the room knocked the words back down her throat. It was filled with moaning, itching and scratching junkies. She had recently relieved her own itch with a pinky nail full up each nostril.

"I'm here," she replied somewhat sympathetically. Luckily, she had never felt the pain of full fledged withdrawals since she kept a steady supply.

"Sissy, come here!" Nick called and breathed new life to a junkie who seemed to be near death. She hopped up and hurdled a few junkies on her way into the kitchen.

"It can take a two," Buella suggested but Nick still gave the junkie a hit straight from the bag. They watched with muted awe mixed with disgust as the woman fixed a fix and ran it into a vein and straight into her soul.

"Uughhhhh!" the woman gasped and fell out in the kitchen.

"Perfect!" Nick cheered when she began to convulse. The junkies in the next room heard the familiar thud of a body dropping and lined up. The flopping around was even better. He hoped she died so word would spread even quicker.

"What about her?" Buella asked as foam began to bubble out of her mouth.

"She'll come to in a few," Nick shrugged like it was no big deal. He served the hungry addicts who scurried into the next room to shoot up as well.

"Oh, ok," she replied and headed for the door. "Call me when you need me..."

"Check," Nick agreed and watched her leave. "Hey Danny, you wanna make a free bag?"

"Ion get down like that!" the junkie shot back. He had

sold, traded, and lost everything in life except for his dignity.
"Get one of these hoes to suck it!"

"Nigga!" Nick shot back at the gay implications. He too
had lost most of his morals too but held on to his heterosexu-
ality. "I'm talking about taking Sissy 'outa here!"

"Oh, ok. Hell yeah!" Danny laughed. He wouldn't suck a
dick but had no problem dumping a body in an alley.

～

"Wow, just wow..." Buella remarked as she recounted
the stacks of cash. She reached the end of the last
batch she mixed and had a dilemma to deal with.

On one hand she was way up and could quit. Graduation
was weeks away now and she could have a lazy summer before
bearing off to college. Her good grades had gotten her
accepted to every college she applied to around the state. Big
Mama was pining for LSU while Ethyl suggested another
college right there in town.

She had also applied for an HBCU in Atlanta that
welcomed her as well. It was so far away from her family and
everyone she knew but that only added to the appeal. She was
leaning towards leaving but was also leaning off the last hit of
heroin she snorted.

"Mph..." Buella grunted when she came out of the nod.
She knew what she had to do but that's always the easy part.
Actually doing it was the hard part. She could and should quit
selling and using but still counted out the cash to re-up and
headed out.

Buella had locked Sadie's sim card trying to get into the
phone after she died so she couldn't call. Still, she had been
with her to Pierre's house enough to know the way. Also

enough not to be a stranger when the doorman looked through the peephole.

"That's lil mama that be with ole girl," the doorman relayed as he looked to see who rang the bell unannounced. Pierre positioned himself in the middle of suburbia to prevent anyone from just happening to be in the neighborhood.

"You may as well just open the damn door because, who the fuck is ole girl who be with lil mama?" Pierre shot back frustrated. Good help was hard to find so his shooter had to answer doors as well and that obviously wasn't his strong point.

"Her!" he replied as he opened the door for Buella.

"Really?" Pierre laughed minus the mirth. He was more shocked than amused to see the girl even though he recognized the bag in her hand. It was the same one Sadie carried to bring cash and take drugs.

"Sorry I ain't call..." Buella offered and held up the bag to explain the rest.

"You ain't had enough of this street life?" Pierre wondered since he could smell she wasn't about this life. She was a baby, and he could smell Similac and mashed peas all the way across the room.

"Ain't had enough of making money," Buella replied and lifted her chin above his scrutiny.

"Just cuz I hate for you to waste a trip..." he said and nodded to his help. He waited for the man to collect the bag and take it away before continuing. "This it tho. Don't brang yo ass 'round here no 'mo!"

"So, my money ain't good after tonight?" Buella dared since she understood everyone did what they did for the money.

"Naw. Hell naw," he replied emphatically as the doorman

returned with the stone-faced woman from before behind him. "It's good?"

"Two times," the woman replied and looked Buella up and down. Her lip curled like the girl had an odor before heading back where she came from.

"Here you go lil mama," the doorman replied and handed the bag back. It felt the same weight as the cash, but she could multiply the money many times over.

"Last time," Pierre repeated as she collected her re-up. "Don't brang yo ass round here no 'mo!"

"Last time..." she agreed and turned to leave. Getting cut off came as a relief since she wasn't sure if she could stop herself on her own. She could feel the eyes on her as she headed out the door and got back into her truck.

Buella's mind was all over the place as she drove back out to Sadie's apartment. It bounced around from Atlanta at the college, to Central City with her sisters and back to the ninth ward where her customers lived. Everywhere but the present, which is how she missed the stop sign she rolled through.

"The fuck?" Buella fussed when she saw the flashing lights behind her. She assumed they were heading to a call somewhere so she slowed and pulled aside so they could pass. Except they didn't pass and pulled behind her. "Shit!"

A million thoughts ran through Buella's head while the cop in the cop car behind her ran the plates. It would come back to Eleanor Fontenot and that could be good or bad depending on which team the cop played for. He made sure there were no wants or warrants before stepping out of his car and approaching.

"License and registration..." he barked and ran his flashlight through the vehicle. He stopped on the bag and tilted his head. Buella contemplated jumping out and making a run for it but managed to stay cool.

"Can I ask what I did officer?" she asked and complied.

"You can," he shot back sarcastically but it was wasted since she didn't catch it. The quip was lost so he explained, "You ran a stop sign back there."

"Where?" she asked and turned around to see if she could see it. "I didn't see it."

"Good thing it wasn't a child playing," he replied and tapped the top of the car, "Hold tight, I'll be right with you."

'Uh-oh!' Buella thought to herself since cops always say that in the movies before they take you to jail. 'Run!' her brain screamed but she didn't budge. She braced herself when the cop got back out of his car and came back.

"Here you go," he said and returned the license. She was clean so by every law in the land she was free to go.

"Thanks," Buella replied and put the registration back into the glove box. She watched his light run through the interior once more and once again settle on the bag containing the next twenty years of her life.

"Can I ask you what's in the bag?" the cop asked offhandedly.

"Yes," Buella replied. The cop scrunched his face at the sarcasm until he realized it wasn't. This little, black girl was as goofy and clueless as the little, white one he was raising at home. Definitely not a criminal carrying enough pure heroin to kill a bunch of people.

"Have a nice night and pay attention to the signs," he said and tapped the hood again before walking away.

"I will officer," she called after him. Buella was the smart sister though and caught the message. This was a sign in itself, and it was time to stop. "After this, I'm done!"

∼

"**S**hit..." Buella fussed when she began to prepare her product for market.

She didn't have nearly enough cut to thin the pure heroin to street level. This was the last go so she would make do. She added the heroin to the grinder and hit the switch. Her feet tapped in anticipation of her favorite part. Once it was broken down, she popped the lid and inhaled the puff of dust from the grinder.

"Mm-mm," Buella moaned as she leaned back to enjoy the rush. Then nodded forward and drifted away.

"Whew!" she reeled when she came back around. "Ok, where was I..."

Buella lost track of pure dope versus harmless cut as she weighed and bagged the heroin. It came out just over half of what she would usually make but didn't have a problem with the short. She was never in this for the money since she had plenty from her grandmother. The street level dealers usually put more steps on it anyway so it should be ok. Should be...

"Sooner I'm done, the sooner I'm done," she reasoned and made her calls to make her rounds. She held a few bags back for her personal use until she quit because she planned to quit using as well.

"Ooh-wee!" Scooter cheered when he saw the product. The color and smell alone told him the story. He promptly paid for it and doubled it by adding an equal amount of cut.

The same thing played out with Black who was just as happy to see the superior product. It was even better than the last bag, so he added even more cut than Scooter had. Both came from the late Wayne's school of thought and could give a fuck how high a junkie got as long as they got paid.

"I'ma be ready again in a day or two," Black informed as he completed his purchase.

SA'ID SALAAM

"Fa sho," Buella said like Sadie used to say. She traipsed out and headed for her last stop for the night.

Buella parked in front of Nick's spot and gathered his order. Her head was down and didn't see the shadow approaching until she opened her door. Once her foot touched the pavement, she felt the cold steel of a gun pressed to her head.

"Come off that bag bitch!" the man growled and pressed the barrel into her flesh hard enough to hurt.

"Here!" Buella moaned and held up the bag. She recognized one of the robbers through the bandana covering his mouth. She knew the name even before she heard it called.

"Fall back Malcolm," Nick demanded from his porch. He didn't have to yell since the laser site in his face spoke loud enough.

"Nigga fuck y..." was as far as Malcolm got before Nick tugged the trigger. The bullet sped into his mouth and splattered the rest of the thought all over Buella and her truck.

"Argh!" the second robber shouted and turned his gun on Nick. Both let loose and sent a volley of bullets speeding towards each other. The result looked like a dance contest as the rounds tore into torsos.

The next thing Buella knew she was the only person alive. She stood there blinking the sudden violence into perspective as the warm blood on her face began to get cold. Her brain told her to leave but her feet were too heavy to move.

"Go! Get out of here!" a familiar voice warned and unfroze the girl. Buella turned and scrunched her face while trying to process the face looking back at her.

"Mama?" she reeled and tilted her head. Her rapid blinks made her mother look like a vintage movie before they had sound.

"Yes baby! You got to get out of here! Go!" Malva urged as

44

she came closer. She had been coming for a fix when she witnessed the stick up gone wrong. The routine robbery was now a murder scene and her daughter needed to flee. Then, she saw the bag clutched in her hand. "I'll hold this. Go on, get!"

"Ok mama," Buella said and snapped out of it. She passed her mother the bag and Malva disappeared before Buella could get seated inside.

"Shit!" Buella fussed when she caught a glimpse of herself in the rearview mirror. She wiped at the blood, but it only smeared since it had begun to dry. She couldn't, wouldn't walk up in the house like that so she changed directions and headed back to Sadie's apartment.

Once inside she stripped off the blood splattered clothing on her way to the shower. She and Sadie had shared many intimate moments in this same space. They used the hand-held showerhead to pleasure each other but now it sent black blood swirling down the drain.

Buella knew she dodged another bullet tonight and had to wonder how many lives she had left. She didn't bother drying or dressing before curling up under the comforter and drifting off to sleep.

CHAPTER SIX

"Shit!" Buella fussed when she awoke the next morning. It took a few seconds to get her bearings and separate fact from fiction. She sorted the memory from her dreams and determined Nick was dead. That part was real and now she had to get home.

Buella lifted her head above the urge for a bump of powder as she dressed and headed down to her car. She didn't notice the bullet hole in her windshield last night, but it was plain as day in the light of day. As was the blood splashed on the side of the truck

"Shit!" she repeated when she opened the door and saw the path the bullet took straight through the headrest.

Buella drove in a daze from the close call. Even as the nagging monkey on her back began to whine. It began to really hoop and holler when she pulled into a self-service car wash. The prissy girl had never washed a car before but knew she couldn't go home like that.

"Wash yo car?" a junkie offered as he appeared from thin

air. Most junkies are actually part magician since they could make shit disappear right before your eyes.

"Huh? Yeah. I got you a few dollars," she replied and stumbled over to the bench. The withdrawals increased and doubled her over. Her skin crawled and stomach churned as she curled into a ball. She knew she couldn't go home like that either and remembered the personal stash she set aside.

Buella popped up to retrieve it from the truck and noticed the truck was empty and the junkie was nowhere in sight. Her head shook as she made her way over. The open glove compartment explained why the junkie had run off without finishing the job. He found her stash and scurried off to get high.

"Fuck!" Buella screamed but it didn't help. Her stomach churned once more and expelled everything from inside. The only thing that kept it from being even worse was her purse draped over her shoulder. Big Mama often said wasn't nothing money can't fix and she had a purse full.

"Sup?" Scooter asked when he opened his door to see a frazzled Buella on his porch. If he didn't know any better, he would have sworn she was fiending like the other dope fiends who came knocking.

"You still straight?" she demanded and walked in on top of him.

"Yeah, I just copped from you last night," he reminded and scrunched his face.

"Give me a sack. Two!" she insisted and produced her cash. Scooter looked back and forth between her and the money until it registered. Then ran his eyes up and down her fine frame.

"Shit, you ain't gotta spend no bread with me lil mama... " he advised and wiggled his brows.

"Um, ok," Buella cheered naively and accepted the two

bags of skag. It was the going rate for pussy around here, but she didn't know any better. "Thanks."

"Wait, I'm saying..." Scooter called after her as she quickly departed with her free dope. It was nothing but God who directed her to the watered-down sacks of the same dope she put out on the street.

Because the junkie who stole her pack was staring off into the afterlife right now with the syringe still stuck in his arm. Buella snorted a bag right there in the driveway but didn't go into a nod. The heavily diluted bag got the monkey off her back but nothing more. She started her truck and headed home where more drama awaited.

~

"What now..." Buella wondered when she made it home.

The men usually ducked and turned away whenever any of Big Mama's precious granddaughters were in sight. Buck disappeared after remarking how fine one of them was so now they didn't look their way. Except today when all eyes were on the girl as she stepped out. She had done so much lately she could only wonder which dirty deed had them staring. She knew the answer was inside, so she headed into the house.

"Where the hell have you been all damn night!" Buella's mother barked. Buella actually flinched for a moment until she realized that wasn't actually her mother.

"None your business lil girl!" she shot back at Lil Baby and turned for the hall.

"Uh, where have you been?" Big Mama fussed but didn't wait for an answer. It wasn't like wherever she had been would change what happened.

"Mama dead,'" Bella chimed in with a look of confusion

49

on her face. She was pretty sure she was supposed to feel something, but nothing came. The neglect acted like novocaine and numbed their senses.

Lil Baby rushed over and hugged her big sister for comfort. She was the only one who shed a tear for the wayward woman. An uncomfortable silence was punctuated by the girl's sobs.

"I just saw..." Buella began but switched gears since that revelation would put her at a triple homicide scene. "I mean how? What happened?"

"What you think?" Bella fussed and rolled her eyes. Being mad was easier than sad so she rolled with it.

"Overdosed. Someone put out some bad product over in ninth ward. Had six overdoses last night. Your mama was just one of them," Big Mama explained.

"Not bad meaning bad but bad meaning good," Ethyl added since she knew whoever had that killer bag was going to make a killing. Literally and physically since junkies' flock to the deadly batches. They wanted to get high enough to knock on heaven's door. Even if it landed them in hell.

"Wow," Buella gasped and stumbled back until she plopped onto the sofa. She knew her mother got the deadly dope from her but wasn't sure if she was sad or mad. The woman was supposed to hold it, not use it. Now her whole investment was in the wind.

Malva actually had good intentions when she took the dope from her daughter. She was still a junkie though so taking a hit from the batch was mandatory. A holding fee but she was so used to the watered-down bags the nearly pure shit killed her before she could pull the needle from her vein. None of the junkies who died had lived long enough to even remove the needle from their arm and that's more valuable than a Super Bowl commercial.

Another junkie witnessed the overdose and pulled the syringe from her arm. Only to load it again from the stash she found in the bag she clutched. She shot the same amount and got the same result. She fell right on top of Malva and died. That set off a deadly Soul Train line as the pack passed from the dead to the living to the dead. It would float around the hood like a mini hurricane sweeping junkies into emergency rooms and morgues until it was depleted.

"Nick dead too," Bella added while Buella was deep in her own head. "Him, Malcolm and Abraham!"

"Malcolm," Buella sighed and shook her head. She clearly recognized the boy she grew up with behind the mask when he tried to rob her. She couldn't stop the corner of her mouth from moving up into a smirk at him getting what he got. A knock at the door came as a welcome distraction.

"Come on..." Big Mama called since only one person would be knocking.

"Hey Big Mama. I need to show you something," Juice said and cut his eyes over at Buella.

"Oh Lawd," she sighed and stood. She didn't view Malva's death as necessarily bad news but knew whatever this was, wasn't good. She looked at Buella as she followed her security man out the house.

"Look like lil mama was in the line of fire?" Juice said and pointed at the bullet hole in Buella's windshield.

"Shit!" her grandmother said with a shiver when she saw the hole in the headrest. The bullet would have gone right into the girl's face had she been seated inside. She turned to the house and roared, "Buella!"

"You in trouble," Lil Baby whispered, wide eyed. She knew their grandmother best since she spent the most time with her. So, she heard the heat in her tone that spelled trouble.

"Prolly," Buella sighed and headed back out of the door.

"What happened here?" Big Mama wanted to know. She already knew the girl's habit of looking up and left when she was about to make something up so she shut that down when she did. "Un-uh! No, you don't! Tell me what happened!"

"I was in the old neighborhood, and they started shooting," she revealed. The truth came easy enough to sound good even if she left out half of the story.

"I don't want you in ninth ward no more!" Big Mama boomed.

"Ok," Buella pouted and hoped that was the end of it.

"Go on back in the house. Don't worry about your mama's funeral. I'ma take care of it..." Big Mama said to her back as she headed inside. Once the door was closed, she turned back to her help. "Find out what really happened."

"On it!" Juice nodded and headed out to do just that.

～

"How I look?" Lil Baby asked but Bella was too busy in the mirror to look.

"You good," she replied and puckered her glossy lips. Then turned to the side to see how her ass was hitting in the black dress. Funeral or no funeral she still wanted to look good. She and Chad were still flirting, playing cat and mouse but it was just a matter of time before he got the kitty.

"You suck!" Lil Baby fussed when her sister refused to share her attention with herself. Luckily Buella walked in, so she asked her, "How I look?"

"Well, damn!" Buella reeled as if she noticed her for the first time. She usually wore regular jeans and shirts but seeing her in the black dress with her black hair cascading around the exposed cleavage shined a new light on the teen. A spotlight and she looked damn good in it. The outburst caused Bella to give the mirror a break and look.

"Damn girl! Where you get them from!" she asked and poked the mound of flesh protruding from the cut in the dress.

"Where she get that ass from!" Buella wanted to know as she turned sideways herself to get a look at her own.

"Mmhm," Lil Baby hummed and nodded. She wouldn't say it, but Buck was right and she was well on her way to be finer than both of her sisters.

Their grandmother saw something else in the girl that she didn't see in her sisters. Which was why she spent the school year schooling her on the family business. Big Mama now let her sit directly in on meetings of the mind with Ethyl instead of running her off to listen from the hallway. The girl knew her place and never spoke unless asked. Then offered a different perspective than the older ladies thought of.

"Y'all girls ready?" Big Mama asked softly as she poked her head in. She too was dressed in all black designer labels, but she was the only one who understood the gravity of the day. Because she had to bury her own mother years back. Life is never the same after watching the casket close on your mother.

"Yes ma'am," the girls sang in a wonderful harmony. Big Mama had siblings once upon a time and knew it was just a matter of time until they would be singing solo.

Buella would be the first to fly the coop since she decided on school in Atlanta. She made excuses and came up with reasons why she wanted to go away for school instead of staying local. Valid sounding excuses but the words between the lines were loud and clear. She needed to get away from New Orleans in the worst way.

Bella's future was less clear since she blew with the wind.

She could end up anywhere from five kids with six baby daddies or CEO of a Wall Street company. Or porn star like her aunt Beatrice out west. Her good looks would be a blessing or a curse. Just depended on which way the wind blew.

Meanwhile Big Mama had big plans for Lil Baby. She was a boss in the making and that was exactly what she was grooming her for. Now way did she build a powerful crime family to turn it over to non-family when one of the two inevitables came calling. The prison and graveyard both beck-oned and it was a race to see who would claim her first.

CHAPTER SEVEN

"Wow!" Bella exclaimed down at the woman in the casket.

"She's so pretty!" Lil Baby agreed since she had never seen Malva all dolled up before. Buella looked away for several reasons, but guilt was the least of them. She blamed her mother for using the drugs instead of her carelessness that put several people in the dirt.

"They did a good job!" Ethyl remarked as she and Big Mama stood back to let the girls spend a few moments with their mama before the proceedings proceeded. ironically this was the longest the woman stood still for her girls in a long time.

"They charged me extra," she sighed since the streets had done so much damage to the woman. The streets were hard enough but the heroin was a wrecking ball. It tore through generations creating junkies and dealers out of nephews and cousins. Mothers, fathers, and grandparents fell victim to one side or the other.

The preacher poked his head out and saw the family had

assembled. Malva's junkie friends wouldn't be attending so he came out and commenced to preaching. Lil Baby listened proudly as the man sung her praises from the script provided by Big Mama. She knew the woman before the streets claimed her and recalled the good in her. Including trying to make a man out of that bitch of a boy she raised.

Malva was once a good mother and was the link between the girls and their grandmother even when Charles forbade it. Big Mama knew her bitch ass son drove her to drugs and out of the house. Weak men have been the destruction of women since the beginning of time. She even blamed Adam for allowing the devil to even speak to his woman in the first place. Men are supposed to be the protectors and maintainers of women, but he failed.

Lil Baby cheesed proudly upon hearing her mother's accolades before becoming a junkie. By the time the preacher reached his last 'amen,' she felt like she knew the woman better in death than she would in life. A light rain fell as they made their way out to the graveyard to put the woman in the ground.

"Are you ok?" Ethyl wondered when she watched Buella shift uncomfortably.

"Cramps," she replied since her monthly minstrel always made a good scapegoat. Aunt Flow took the blame for lots of things from lots of women over the years. She was a good excuse to get out of a lot of different things.

"Hmp..." the woman wondered. She was post menopausal but had enough periods in her lifetime to know this was more than that. She had gotten to know the older girls through driving them to and fro for most of the school year. The back of her mind suggested the right answer, but it just didn't make much sense.

"What?" Big Mama asked when she saw the troubled look

on her friend's face. She knew the woman too well for her to pass it off as nothing. Ethyl nodded at Buella, and her grandmother began to keep an eye on her as well.

'Put some dirt on her already...' Buella moaned inwardly as the casket finally began to lower. Her skin was crawling, and stomach tumbled like a dryer filled with wet clothes. The grease from the heavy breakfast Big Mama cooked bubbled inside her belly until it came bubbling out her mouth.

"Ewwww!" Bella fussed and made faces while Lil Baby was more sympathetic.

"You ok?" the youngest sister inquired and pressed the back of her hand to Buella's forehead to check for a temperature.

"Oh, hell naw!" Big Mama moaned woefully. Had it been Bella throwing up again she would have known she was pregnant.

Buella didn't date boys but was dealing with the drug dealing girl. This could only be one thing and she knew it. Sadie escaped a painful death through death because Big Mama was boiling mad. She would personally have murdered the girl if she wasn't already dead. Which made Sadie the first person in history to be lucky to be dead.

"Hmp," Ethyl huffed since she had her suspicions for a while. "What we gonna do?"

"I'ma take her out to the swamp..." Big Mama decided on the spot. Ethyl's eyes went wide at the thought of her feeding the girl to Ole George. Big Mama read her mind and shook her own head. "Chile please..."

"Where are we going?" Buella wanted to know as Big Mama pulled out the driveway. "How long we gonna be gone?"

"Until we get back!" Big Mama shot back, then reeled herself in. As upset as she was, it needed to be directed towards herself. This happened on her watch and now she had to fix it. "We haven't spent any girl time in a minute!"

"Cuz you're always with Lil Baby," Buella pouted. It was the first time she admitted to herself that she was slightly jealous. Still, she had more pressing matters on her mind. Her body shifted in the passenger seat as she fought the withdrawals setting in and taking hold.

"Well, granny is going to make it up. I'm gonna make it all better," she vowed and sighed.

"Ok, cuz I have a, supposed to go, we have to..." Buella stammered in search of an excuse to go get high. Even if the weak work on the streets was only enough to get her off sick. Which was why the hardcore junkies shot it directly into their veins. They shot two and three times the normal amount. Which was why they dropped dead when a real pack hit the streets.

"Don't worry, Big Mama finna fix it..." Big Mama assured as her granddaughter curled into a fetal ball to hold herself together. The cityscape gave way to countryside as they headed for New Iberia.

~

"You coming Bella?" Lil Baby asked after changing out of the funeral dress. She liked how she looked all dressed up but preferred her jeans and T-shirt any day.

"Naw, I'm just gonna rest. I'm not in the mood," Bella

pouted. It sounded reasonable since she just buried her mother.

"You sure? We finna eat up some shit!" Ethyl laughed. She knew the girl could definitely eat. She was young enough to get away with it for now.

"Yeah, just bring me some beignets. Please," she asked and added another sigh.

"We got you," Lil Baby assured since she had her own money to buy it. She hugged her sister's neck before following Ethyl out the door.

"I'm with y'all," Juice advised when the women stepped out. He noticed they were one short and asked, "Where's the other one?"

"Inside moping. She staying," Ethyl advised.

"Hmp?" Juice huffed and looked over to Chad. He had no choice but to leave him behind to watch the girl but felt like he was leaving a chicken hawk in the hen house. Then again, the remaining girl did just bury her mother so she was probably grieving.

"I got it boss," Chad assured and puffed his chest to show he was up for the task.

"Mmph," Juice huffed and hopped in his car to trail the females in the lead car. Making sure nothing happened to Ethyl and Lil Baby was more pressing than making sure Bella didn't fuck.

Chad watched the cars until they were out of sight. Then the front door swung open with Bella in booty shorts and T-shirt tied into knot to show off her hard stomach. He shook his head and headed inside.

Bella jumped into his arms and shoved her tongue into his mouth. He wasn't as good a kisser as Thibodeaux but gripped her ass as he held her up just like he used to do. His fingers found their way under the tiny shorts and reached her juicy box.

"Mm-mm," Bella moaned when he slid a finger inside of her. She felt his knees buckle when she squeezed and clamped her hot box around the finger. That made getting inside the girl the most important thing in the world.

Chad used one hand to drop his pants while still holding her up with the other. Bella assisted by tugging the shorts to the side as he wriggled the head of his dick inside of her. She hissed and moaned as she sank onto the dick filling her insides. They began to fuck right there in the living room.

Bella bucked her hips as he lifted and dropped her on the dick. It was a pretty good stroke, but she was way too slick, slippery, and tight to last too long at this rate. Chad felt his knees buckle again just before he exploded inside of her.

"Un-uh!" Bella protested but not about him coming inside of her. She was destined for a bunch of babies or abortions but in the meanwhile wanted to get fucked properly.

"My bad lil mama," Chad apologized. He was just seventeen, so he stayed hard as a tree trunk. He waddled down the hall with his pants at his ankles and her in his arms. Then dropped her on her bed and fucked her properly.

~

"Here we are baby," Big Mama groaned as they made their way down the bumpy, dirt road. Seeing her grandchild curled up in pain was almost as bad as the moans that escaped her mouth.

"Here where?" Buella wondered when she opened an eye. All she saw were pine trees passing the window until the car stopped.

"Here," she repeated and popped the trunk. Big Mama

had done a little shopping and loaded the necessities into the trunk. She would make a second trip to collect them once she handled her business inside.

"I really need to get back to the city..." Buella pleaded as they walked into the small house. The smell of souls reached her as soon as they stepped inside. The place had been bleached and sanitized after each use, but bleach can't clean spilled souls.

"I know girl," her grandmother assured and guided her to the middle of the room. Buella tilted her head at the odd sliding doors to nowhere as Big Mama knelt below. She heard the 'click' of the cuff around her ankle before looking down and seeing it.

"What's that?" Buella asked but Big Mama was heading out the door. "Hey! What are you doing! Where you going!"

"Hush chile," Big Mama fussed when she returned with the supplies. Buella hushed to watch as she sat a bag down and began unloading it. First came the plastic bucket and explanation.

"You finna shit and piss. Best to do it here than in your clothes," she explained. Next came the gallons of water that really needed no explanation. Then her favorite candy bars since she wasn't going to be able to keep any food down. Buella was indeed the smart sister and quickly figured out what was going on.

"Grammaw, I ain't no junkie! Swear 'fo gawd I ain't!" she pleaded and crossed her heart.

"I know baby," she replied and scrunched her face to figure out how to work the pump on the air mattress. "I got you a radio..."

"I don't want no fuck ass radio! Turn me loose! You crazy lady!" Buella yelled and pulled at the cuff. Big Mama recalled her own son tugging at the cuff until his ankle bled. Buella suddenly stopped when she saw the look in the woman's eyes.

"This for your own good," she sighed and continued removing the heedless knickknacks from the bag. None of it accounted for much since Buella was born with what she needed to slay this dragon. She proved it by taking the abuse she took from her father. She seemed to know it too and lifted her chin.

"I'll be through tomorrow to check on you. It's up to you how long you stay here," she advised. Buella lifted her chin defiantly when the woman leaned in to kiss her cheek. She waited until she was gone before breaking down. Plenty of tears had been shed in this house. Along with blood and sweat. She would lose those fluids too but if she survived, she would be the first to make it out alive.

CHAPTER EIGHT

Big Mama was watching her favorite drama show when she felt the eyes on the back of her head. Only one person in the house moved with that sort of stealth so she continued watching the murder and mayhem of the world news. When the intruder hadn't spoken by commercial, she spoke up in hopes of having whatever this conversation was before the news resumed.

"What chile?" she asked behind her.

"Did you kill my sister?" Lil Baby snarled as she came around. The tone in her voice made Big Mama glance to her hands to make sure they were empty. She knew the child was fierce and was glad it extended the protection to her sisters.

Bella was too busy getting dicked down to worry about her sister being gone for two days. She used her money to bribe Lil Baby out of the house with food or movies since Ethyl and Juice would have to take her. That left her and Chad home alone to fuck every which way but loose. They had every kind of sex except safe sex in every room of the house except Big Mama's room. That definitely wouldn't be safe.

"Why the hell would I kill my granddaughter!" Big Mama fussed like it was the most ludicrous question she had ever heard. It actually was but according to Lil Baby's next statement, reasonable.

"You killed Charles," she reasoned. The word father or dad never could come so she settled for his given name.

"Shole did, because he hurt you. Hurt y'all. And I will kill the whole world before I let anyone, or anything hurt y'all!" Big Mama declared and ignored the news coming back from the commercial.

"So where is she?" the girl dared and cocked her head. She listened for a lie since she already knew the truth.

"She is sick. I took her out to the house to heal," she nodded at how the PG-13 answer sounded. It rolled off the tongue smoothly enough to sound true, so the girl bought it. "I'm finna go check on her in a few."

"I wanna come!" Lil Baby insisted and lifted her chin.

"No!" Big Mama shot back ferociously. It would definitely be a deterrent to deter her against drug use, but Big Mama knew that would never be her problem. Lil Baby's issues in life would be the flashes of anger she saw in the girl from time to time. If it ever got the best of her, it would do her in.

"Tell her I said Hey!" she settled since it was clear she wasn't going.

Deterrent or not it was an ugly sight to see. She let out a deep sigh as she stood to go check the girl as she had over the last few days. This was a battle that had to be fought solo, so she left Buella to fight.

"I'll tell her you said Hey," she sighed. Then turned her cheek to accept the kiss the girl was bringing.

"Give that to my sister!" Lil Baby sang and skipped away down the hall.

"Ion know about all that..." Big Mama sighed since she knew what to expect when she got there. She gathered her strength and made the drive out to the swamp. It was easier riding out to murder her son than seeing her grand baby in the clutches of withdrawals.

Her heavy heart made her feet t light since she was in no hurry to see what awaited. She made the usual stops for the usual supplies but added another stop tonight. The dirt road seemed a lot shorter tonight and got her to the house before she was ready.

"Lawd, give me strength..." she moaned and entered the house. Having known what to expect still didn't prepare Big Mama for what she heard. The moans and groans seeped through the door but suddenly stopped when she stepped inside.

Buella was butt naked with a sheen of sweat covering her body. Her hair had drawn up into a curly fro and she looked pale and gaunt. She had rubbed her ankle raw and bloody from pulling against the cuff. It would leave a scar as a reminder of this ordeal, if she lived through it.

The two women cocked their heads at each other but didn't speak. Big Mama ignored the stench of the bucket as she replaced it with a new one. She slid the door open and tossed the vile piss, shit, vomit and bile into the swamp. Critters rushed forward to investigate, then quickly dispersed at the unsavory introduction.

"Hmp," Big Mama huffed at the empty water bottles. Today she introduced a plate of home cooked stew along with ice cold Gatorade. She heard the girl's stomach growl loudly when she saw the food, but Buella didn't budge. She did accept the box of Wet wipes to clean herself.

"How long do I gotta stay here?" Buella asked as her grandmother finished the routine she had done over the last few days.

"That's up to you," she replied and pulled out a bag of dope. They both looked down at it, then up to each other. Big Mama sat it next to the food and turned to leave. She could hear the crinkle of the package as he headed out the door. Her head shook but she didn't speak. She waited until she was back in her car before she broke down crying.

~

"Hey grammaw!" Lil Baby cheered when Big Mama walked back in the house. She was always happy to see the woman but was expecting to see her sister coming in behind her.

"Naw she's not with me, and naw I ain't killed the girl!" Big Mama groaned.

"Did she..." Ethyl began but stopped short since Lil Baby was in her mouth.

"Girl yes," Big Mama replied and twisted her lips at the sound of the package opening when she left the house. It was a gamble and she lost. The setback would knock Buella's rehab back to day one. Footsteps up the hall came as a relief from the morbid reality.

"I need to tell you something grandmother," Bella announced.

"Ain't we formal!" the woman laughed, happy to be happy.

"I want you to know that me and Chad are in love! We want to be able to date!" she proclaimed.

"We been knew that," Lil Baby sighed and rolled her eyes.

"We did," Big Mama nodded.

"Knew it before you did prolly," Ethyl added and joined

the laughter. Bella said what she said and turned back down the hall. The laughter left with her, and the women had some business to tend to.

"What did you find out about the source of my problem?" Big Mama asked over to her sidekick.

"Pierre. She and that other chile been shopping with him for a minute," Ethyl replied. That much was previously known but cast in a different light now that Buella had actually been using.

"Hmp..." the woman huffed in thought. She actually liked Pierre in a nephew sort of way since she knew his uncle once upon a time. He still sold her the drugs that got her granddaughter hooked and she needed someone to blame.

"He is in the way anyway," Ethyl added, which was the equivalent of a thumbs down in gladiator days. Pierre had a nice piece of the heroin sales in the city. It may have been personal for the boss, but it was a good business move as well.

"I guess I should send Jazzy-belle to say hey," Big Mama sighed. This would kill two birds with one stone since she could take over Pierre's market once he was gone. Because the notorious Jazzy-belle sent people bye-bye went she said Hey.

"Hmp," Ethyl huffed to show what she thought of using the sadistic woman to do their dirty work.

They had a team of men who could and would kill on command. A shiver ran up her spine at the very mention of the woman. Lil Baby looked back and forth between the two women and soaked up the unspoken lesson. She watched her grandmother mull over the suggestion, then shrug and overruled it.

"Sometimes too much is just enough," Big Mama declared and his fate was sealed. Ethyl pursed her lips but that would be the end of her protest. Meanwhile Pierre had a date with destiny.

~

"Hey nah!" Pierre cheered and tossed dollars at the woman twerking in front of him. He made thousands of dollars each day and tricked off a few hundred every night. He was 'easy come, easy go' in the flesh because he liked to spend his money on flesh.

"Good googly moogly!" New York exclaimed when he spotted the jet-black beauty slink into the bar. The Senegalese and East Indian mix of features gave the woman an exotic look that stood out in any room she stepped in. The smooth, black skin with the long, black hair and deep, dark eyes turned heads. If anyone could see inside of her black heart they would run from, not to the woman.

"Sheeet..." Pierre announced and slid from the booth. Jazzy-belle had just entered the bar but by the time she reached a bar stool the man was by her side. "Yo money ain't no good chere! Order whatever you want!"

"Hmp," she huffed and looked him up and down. Not only did he look like money, but he also looked just like the man in the picture on her phone. "Pierre..."

"You know my name so what's yours? Why I ain't never seen you around chere?" he asked, sizing her up as well. She stood a tall five foot, nine inches with nice mounds of black, titty meat protruding from the top of her dress.

"I'll be whoever you need me to be," she replied and turned to the side to help him look her over.

"Damn girl!" Pierre exclaimed when he saw how far her ass jetted out from her small waist. "Like I said, whatever you want! A Charger? BMW..."

"I really just want some dick," she shrugged. The next thing she knew she was being pulled from the bar.

"Say man!" New York shouted when he saw his ride leaving without him. He just shook his head when he saw the look in Pierre's eyes. He would have said more had he known that would be the last time he saw his friend.

"Ion stay too far..." Pierre grunted as he whipped through the city.

"Hurry!" Jazzy-belle groaned and lifted her feet to the dashboard. She pulled her dress up and began making circles on her love button with her fingers.

"Shit!" he shouted when his passenger busted a nut in the passenger seat. It made his foot heavier as he sped home. He barreled up into his driveway so fast he tapped the bumper of his other vehicle when he stopped. He used the key fob to turn on the alarm and rushed his guest inside.

"Whoa, slow down!" Jazzy-belle advised when he moved on her as soon as they crossed the threshold. He would have smashed her at the front door after the display in the car.

"Ok, ok," he nodded in agreement and amazement when she lifted her dress over her head. His eyes blinked in the plump breasts with big, black nipples. Then down to the rippled stomach above the freshly shaved mound hanging between her legs like a ripe papaya. He reached for her vagina just as the silver glint registered in his mind.

"The fuck..." Pierre fussed when he felt the swipe across his neck. Then noticed the straight razor in her black hand.

"Big Mama said to say hey..." she answered the confused look on the man's face. The super sharp blade didn't cause any pain, so Pierre wondered if she missed.

Until the smooth line she made turned white, then burst and sent blood gushing forth. Both severed jugular veins spewed blood like a pump. His open trachea prevented him from saying a word even though he had so much to say as his whole life flashed before his eyes.

Jazzy-belle tilted her head curiously but stepped back so he wouldn't get any blood on her. She really did want some dick before the night was over and dudes don't like chicks with blood all over them. Plus, she had work to do since Big Mama awarded her any spoils she found.

"They usually keep a stash right about..." Jazzy-belle was saying to herself as she opened the dresser drawer. As expected, she found neat stacks of bundled cash. She collected it, the jewelry, and assorted valuables from around the room. Her nose turned up at the drugs she came across since she hated them. It was a love/hate relationship though because the majority of her business came from the drug trade.

"I like this one better," she decided and took the Cadillac Pierre bumped when they pulled in. It would fetch a nice price when she took it home to Baton Rouge. A dude named Kief ran a chop shop specializing in hot wheels just like this.

Her work here was done so she headed home. There was no need to call and report since this one would make the news.

CHAPTER NINE

"I'll be back in a few," Big Mama sighed a frustrated sigh at the heavy task ahead of her. She first laid eyes on Buella minutes after she was born. Mainly to make sure Malva didn't trick her goofy son with a baby. She fell in love with the pretty girl even before the DNA test confirmed she was her blood.

Seeing her in the condition she left her in was painful. She knew the girl would be in even heavier withdrawals after the failed test. Putting more heroin in her system set the clock back to zero. Big Mama noticed movement and saw Lil Baby right behind her. She raised a brow for an explanation.

"I'm going with you," Lil Baby replied and walked by her to the car.

"You can't go with me!" she shot back but the teen hopped into the passenger seat anyway. "Look, lil girl..."

Big Mama paused when her granddaughter buckled her seatbelt and defiantly crossed her arms over her chest. She lifted her chin and looked out the window as if the woman wasn't talking about anything. Big Mama realized this was actually a teaching moment.

Never in a million years did she see Buella using but understood. The girl had to grow up way too fast and had been through way too much. On second thought she would have been more surprised if the girl didn't use. Either way, letting Lil Baby see what drugs do was better than any class she could teach.

Big Mama thought about calling Bella out as well when she saw her peeping through the blinds. She shook her head knowing the girl was just waiting for them to leave so she could sneak Chad into the house. She just shook her head and pulled away.

The ride out to New Iberia was made in silent reflection. Lil Baby needed to see her big sister. This was the longest she had been away from her since she was a little baby. Big Mama was in full Grandma mode, thinking how she could save her grandchild. Oddly enough the thought of how many other families suffered this same affliction at the hands of her own drugs never crossed her mind. As long as it was someone else's family she didn't give a fuck.

"What grammaw?" Lil asked when a smile spread on the woman's face. It didn't match the grisly report coming through the system.

"Who? Naw," Big Mama waved her off and didn't share what parted her lips. Jazzy-belle did her thing and put Pierre on the news. It wasn't much but it was something and something is always better than nothing. The car went silent again until they were halfway down the dirt road.

"What is this place?" the teen asked from the passenger seat. Just as the unique aroma of the swamp seeped into the car.

"This is where we..." Big Mama began but had to find a

new description. For years it was where they took the trash out but that was her baby in there sweating and pissing on herself. "This is where we work things out. Come on..."

Lil Baby's eyes shot in every direction as they walked from the car to the house. The movement of the living swamp stole her attention and stopped her in her tracks. It was only when she heard her sister's voice when the door opened did, she move again. Came running actually.

"Buella!" Lil Baby shrieked and ran smack dab into her big sister while their grandmother dumped the bucket of piss.

"Hey girl!" Buella moaned and squeezed her sister with what strength she had.

"Ewww! You stink!" Lil Baby finally fussed and scrunched her pretty face. It scrunched some more when she saw what she was wearing. "Why you naked? Why you chained?"

"Cuz grammaw," Buella snarled and looked at the woman.

"Tuh!" Big Mama huffed. This was everyone in the world's fault before she would take the blame. She handed her the food she brought and watched as the girl devoured it. Which in itself was a good sign.

"Dang! You must been hungry!" Lil Baby laughed. The smart girl quickly added the bits and pieces she overheard at home with the traces she picked up in the streets and knew why her sister was here. "You gotta get off the dope Buella!"

"I am!" she declared and cocked her head defiantly at their grandmother. "I'm done."

"Tuh!" Big Mama huffed again just before her eyes fell on the package of dope on the floor. She pursed her lips into a 'yeah right' and picked it up. Buella looked even more defiant when the woman saw every crumb of dope was present and accounted for.

"I'm good. On my..." Buella began but remembered she

didn't have a mama to swear by anymore. God was still a life-time away for her, so she only had herself. "I'm good."

"Tuh!" Big Mama huffed one more time but removed the key from her purse. She dropped and saw the wounds healing on her ankle as she un-cuffed her. "We not doing this no more. Next time we just finna find you a pretty dress and lay you next to your mama."

"She not doing it no more!" Lil Baby shouted into her sister's face.

"Naw, we not doing this no more..." Buella replied. She knew she would lay next to her mother if it happened again. She actually preferred it.

"Go get that bag from the trunk!" Big Mama ordered and waited for the girl to leave the house. Lil Baby rushed to retrieve the clothes her grandmother kept for this day. Once she was gone, she turned back to Buella. "I mean it girl, no more!"

"I mean it too," Buella shot back. The dope didn't break her but definitely left a dent. She collected her clothes from her sister when she returned and headed into the shower in the next room. Lil Baby explored the rest of the house while she got cleaned up.

"What the hell!" Lil Baby fussed when she opened the door to nowhere. "What's this for?"

"You'll see soon enough," Big Mama replied and she was right. It was just a matter of time.

∽

"Hey," Bella greeted when her sister walked into the room. She only lifted her head long enough to register her sister's presence, then back down to her phone.

"Dassit?" Buella wondered of the lukewarm greeting.

"My bad," she said and shook it off before running up and squeezing her sister. "You look..."

"Like shit? I feel like shit," Buella admitted. She had shaken that monkey off her back but a junkie is a junkie for life. Even when they stop using. It was an uphill battle, but she was determined to win that battle.

"Let me tell you about Chad!" Bella switched gears since she never liked not being the center of attention.

"Mph! Mmhm! Un-uh!" Buella reacted even if she hardly listened.

The few days she had been gone felt like weeks and she had things to do. Being caught in the fog of drugs set her back months and there were only weeks left of school. She had to get herself back together so she wouldn't be stuck here forever. She had plans and none of them had anything to do with New Orleans.

"You want something from the store?" Lil Baby asked. The only thing she enjoyed more than sending the grown men to the store for her snacks was going herself with them trailing as security. Especially since the pack of girls down the street stared every time, they saw her.

"Naw," Buella replied even though there was plenty she wanted. What she needed most lay between her sheets, so she climbed into the bed and was fast asleep.

Lil Baby and Bella watched her sleep for a few minutes before their own lives called for attention. Bella jumped on the phone to talk dirty while Lil Baby slid down the hall to see what business the Family business was getting into.

"May as well come 'round that corner," Big Mama called when she heard Lil Baby post up in her favorite spot. She always heard her and always let her listen. Lately she invited her to take a seat at the table.

"Hey there Toot," Ethyl greeted out of habit until she saw

how much the girl had filled out recently. "Guess I can't call you toot no 'mo?"

"But you can always call me Lil Baby," she replied.

"You gonna be Lil Baby after you big and grown!" Big Mama cosigned and got down to business. Despite the near tragedy with Buella she was poised to take over the heroin market left by the late Pierre. Unlike Big Mama he didn't have any heirs to leave his drug trade to. That left it up for grabs so Big Mama decided to grab it. "Send a crew over there and soften them up for me to come talk."

"On it," Ethyl nodded and stood to relay the shot she called to send shots. Literally since her gunmen would shoot up the block enough to dissuade anyone from slinging on it. Then send her dope boys with her dope and get it popping.

"Sometimes you can get more bees with honey," Lil Baby suggested softly. All heads turned to her, so she continued. "Them boys prolly want to work with you, not fight."

"Well go on over there and ask them if they want to get down with the winning team," Big Mama nodded in agreement. Ethyl scrunched her face at the odd request since that was clearly a job for Juice. Even he would take a team of shooters just in case negotiations broke down.

"Ok," the girl shrugged and stood.

"Sit your tail down!" Big Mama laughed. Her head lolled bared all her teeth as she had a hearty laugh at the girl's heart. "I swear this girl got more heart then half them niggas out in the yard!"

"More balls than half the men I ever knew," Ethyl added and laughed at the uncomfortable grimace on her face at the notion of having a set of balls.

"Want something from the store?" Lil Baby asked as a way of asking to go to the store.

"Big Mama could use a pack of menthol," Big Mama

decided after squeezing her nearly empty pack. "Oh, and the biggest, fastest, pinkish pickled pig foot in the jar!"

"Ewww! No!" Lil Baby grimaced in disgust. The sounds of the women's laughter carried her out of the house and yard. She heard the men scramble when she walked out of the yard, headed up the block. This was a dangerous city and Big Mama had enemies who had pet pigs and alligators too. Big Mama would do this city worse than Katrina if anything happened to her girls.

"I got it," Chad offered and jumped up. He and Bella were boo loving on the line but that didn't stop him from falling in behind the girl. Hopefully it could earn more points with the fickle teen.

Chad looked down at Lil Baby's spreading ass but quickly turned away. Buck was most likely right, and she was going to be the finest of the Fontenot sisters, but he wasn't going to die about it. Plus, he was utterly in love with the girl fussing in his ear.

"You not even listening to me! Must be some bitch got your attention!" Bella fussed because she thought she was supposed to. Unfortunately, so many women only see bad relationships growing up and have no guide.

"Yeah, I'm listening to you! No, no bitches got my attention!" He lied since he spotted a group of girls headed towards Lil Baby. The pack of ragamuffins saw Lil Baby often and hated her from a distance. Now that she was alone, they made their move. "Hole up, let me hit you back..."

"You must see some bitch! I..." Bella was fussing some more but the line went dead so Chad could protect her sister. Bella was too spoiled to be hung up on and called back. Each time the phone went to voicemail she got even angrier.

"Hey! Who is you!" one girl fussed as they crossed the street. Lil Baby looked her up and down and rolled her eyes.

"Un-uh! She think she cute! Her hair ain't real! I'll scratch her face!" the others added. They ran plenty of pretty girls off their block, but Lil Baby wasn't just pretty, she was with the shits. The hot shit, bull shit, fuck shit and all the shits.

"First of all,..." Lil Baby announced as she stopped to confront them.

"Oh Lawd!" Chad groaned and shook his head.

"I am cute, and I go wherever I want..." she replied and locked eyes with the leader. The ugly little girl with a two-inch ponytail protruding from a dirty scrunchy on her gelled down head. "Touch my face and I'll kill yo ass!"

"Bitch!" the leader shouted like a wild banshee and took off towards her.

"Un-uh!" Chad declared and whipped out his pistol. The large gun stopped the other girls in their tracks, but Lil Baby still wanted smoke.

"Nuh-uh! We finna end this rat chere, rat nah!" she insisted. "One on one! Bring yo ass!"

"You ain't said nothing!" The ugly girl shot back and put up her battle scarred hands. Lil Baby's hands were smooth and deceptively dainty. She balled her yellow fist up and took a fighter's stance.

"Bet not nare one of y'all lil bitches budge!" Chad warned with the gun hanging at his side. The two girls squared off in the middle of the street and prepared for battle.

"Get her Jernika! Beat her ass! Pull her hair out! Scratch her face!" her friends cheered from the sideline. It was only the big gun that prevented them from jumping her and stomping her into the asphalt below.

"Argh!" Jernika screamed and charged. She twirled her hands like a windmill as she ran up. Lil Baby just shook her head since the girl obviously couldn't fight. The windmill style was only effective against other girls using it. They would slap, punch, and scratch each other until someone quit.

Not Lil Baby though, she was Buella and Bella's little sister and knew how to fight. She happily dipped and ducked the slaps, punches and scratches and returned generous jabs and hooks that made the ugly girl even uglier. She soon had two knots on her head that looked like horns. Her nose was leaking, and lips were puffy and busted.

"Un-uh! Beat that bitch!" her friends shouted even though Jernika wanted to quit. She knew she was whooped but couldn't concede. She ran her crew with her muscle and losing here meant losing control. Losing this fight would mean having to fight one or all of them again to hold her spot at the top.

"Ok, that's enough!" Chad said as he stepped in and picked Lil Baby up. Jernika was relieved at the reprieve. Except she was just foul and couldn't take the L with grace. Chad had Lil Baby in the air, so she ran over and took a swipe at her face. Her fingernail carved a nice scratch down her yellow cheek.

"Put me down!" Lil Baby demanded as Jernika ran off and dipped inside of her shotgun house. She may have gotten away, but Lil Baby still wanted to fight. "Come on! I'll fight all y'all hoes!"

"We good. You got that. We cool," they surrendered and backed away.

"Oh Lawd!" Chad replied and groaned when he saw the gash in the girl's face.

"What?" Lil Baby wondered and lifted her hand to the burning in her cheek.

"Nuffin, let's get yo chips 'n-shit so we can go home," he signed. He could only wonder how much trouble he was in for not returning the girl the way he got her. They headed to the store where Lil Baby mixed and matched snacks. She used to only have a dollar to spend but money wasn't an issue now, so she loaded the counter.

"Huh?" Lil Baby asked when she caught a glimpse of herself in the mirror behind the counter. She examined the long gash in the middle of her cheek. The look of horror soon morphed into a smile. "Cool!"

"That's cool?" Chad wondered, wide eyed.

"It's like Buella's!" she recalled and smiled wider. Buella's scar was gone now thanks to Big Mama's doctor, but Lil Baby thought it was cool when she got it. Big Mama would fix hers too but that didn't change the fact that she got it. She had given her word, so she reiterated, "I'm going to kill that bitch"

CHAPTER TEN

"Oh, hell naw!" Big Mama protested when she saw her darling grand baby enter the house. Her hair was wild, and the ugly, red gash stood out on her yellow face.

"What?" she wondered and popped another chip in her mouth. In true hood fashion she placed it on her tongue to savor the flavor before chewing.

"It was some lil gals tryna fight her. I made them shoot a fair one. Lil Baby whooped her ass, but she snuck a scratch in and ran!" Chad explained. Bella heard his voice and ran up the hall.

"What happened to you?" Bella demanded but wasn't talking to her sister. "You hung up on me!"

"Yo sister got to fighting," he explained.

"Well, I knew you was gonna have to fight them girls sooner or later," Ethyl added. "New girls in the neighborhood. Pretty too..."

"Probably think y'all finna take all they little boyfriends!" Big Mama agreed with a hearty laugh.

"Ewww! Don't nobody want they dang boyfriends!" Lil

Baby protested and scrunched her face up worse than she did about the pig's feet.

"Hold that thought!" Big Mama laughed some more.

"Mmhm, keep that same energy!" Ethyl cackled. The girl was blossoming right before their eyes. It was just a matter of time until she bit the apple and noticed boys as much as they noticed her already. The conversation between Chad and Bella stole everyone's attention when it got loud.

"I was helping her! Them girls would have jumped her!" he insisted but Bella wasn't hearing it.

"Then you should have kept me on the line! You don't hang up no phone on me!" Bella shouted. "Dassit! Ion mess with you no 'mo!"

Chad stood there blinking in disbelief as Bella marched back down the hall and into the room. She slammed the door behind her and awoke her sister. Buella was still sleeping off the effects of her trip to the gates of hell and back. She groaned, flipped over, and went back to sleep.

"Guess I better, yeah, I'll just..." Chad muttered as he stepped back outside.

"Next!" Big Mama laughed as the impetuous girl broke up with her boyfriend. Teenage girls fall in and out of love every other day, so no one was surprised. The older ladies had once been teen girls themselves. Not to mention raising one each once upon a time.

"Who does she remind you of?" Ethyl dared but barely got it out of her mouth.

"Un-uh! Don't do me like that!" Big Mama grimaced and shook her head. Truth was, Bella was her daughter Beatrice all over again. She loved the guys just like they loved her. Her beauty was a blessing and a curse that left broken hearts and dead bodies all over New Orleans.

"Who! What?" Lil Baby asked between the two women

but got ignored. She gave up and stomped down the hall and into the bathroom to admire her scar.

~

"This my nephew Cosby," Juice introduced the new face as the men gathered for their mission.

The men all greeted him heartily and happily since he was now one of them. He may or may not have actually been Juice's blood since he called most people his nephew. All the men greeted besides Chad that is since Cosby was a light skin, pretty boy with light eyes and curly hair. Exactly what he didn't want around his girl even though Bella wasn't his girl anymore.

"Sup woadie?" Chad greeted when Cosby shook hands all around. He extended his too but made it sound like a dare when they shook.

"It's whatever with me," Cosby replied to match his energy. Which was weird since they were on the same team. He was being honest though because it really was whatever with him.

"Y'all finna whip out and see who dick longer?" Mook asked when he saw them youngins sizing each other up.

"What we checking for length, or girth?" Juice asked and pulled out some money. The man was known to bet on just about anything including this.

"I'm good?" Cosby literally asked since he had no idea what was going on. He was about to find out when the door opened and the two of the Fontenot sisters stepped out before Big Mama. He instantly passed over Lil Baby since her face looked younger than her body. Then locked on Bella who looked back and locked on.

Cosby was warned before he got herer so he turned away,

only to see the love struck look on Chad's face. He followed his gaze back over to Bella just as she rolled her eyes at Chad and hopped in the passenger seat. Mook was tasked with security for the day since Juice had Family business across town.

"Oooooh!" Cosby laughed when he caught on. A triangle has three parts but he had no intentions on being one of them. He raised his hands in surrender and said, "I got a whole wife back at the house!"

"Whenever y'all done, we can tend to this business," Juice suggested and got into his SUV. Mook moved and slid into the passenger seat while Chad and Cosby shared space in the back seat.

The murderous music coming through the speaker set the tone for the shooters in the back. The men up front hoped for a more diplomatic solution. Bullets and bodies cost money while cooperation pays. He was meeting Pierre's silent partner called Say-So. The moniker was earned since bodies had dropped on his say so.

"Heads up..." Juice announced as they pulled up to the park. He saw Say-So posted up under a pavilion alone but knew he wasn't. His eyes scanned the area for his shooters but didn't see any. A smile spread as he picked his men from the seemingly random folks out and about.

"We can end his ass here and now," Mook said but only because Mook was naive.

"Naw..." Juice replied as the shooters he had been searching for began to manifest. The woman pushing a stroller with a chopper inside. The couple with Mac-11s in their picnic basket. The sorry players on the basketball court who kept cutting their eyes over to the pavilion. "Y'all stay put."

"Stay put?" Chad groaned since he was hoping for some

action. Anything to get Bella's attention so he could get back inside of her.

"Put nigga!" Mook seconded as Juice stepped towards the pavilion. He caught on when he too spotted some of the shooters. He would have popped it off with the men on the court, but the woman would have pulled that chopper from the stroller and sent them to the upper room.

"That guy Juice!" Say-So cheered and stood respectfully as Juice came near.

"Say-So," he replied and extended his hand. Both men locked eyes in search of any inner bitch that might show as they squeezed hands. Neither found any so they released their grip and sat on opposite sides of the table. "Big Mama sends her regards..."

"Fuck that bitch. She kilt my people," Say-So shot back, rather calmly. He had a deadly demeanor without ever raising his voice.

"He was selling dope to her people. Grand baby got strung out on the shit," Juice managed even though he heard how hypocritical it sounded. Plenty of his own people used heroin. Some, the heroin used back and had them working in one of Big Mama's brothels. He knew selling dope requires selling one's soul first and he was ok with it.

"That's personal," Say-So nodded since he was a hypocrite himself. "But taking the work was bad business."

"On God, we ain't take no work!" he shot back. Say-So tilted his head dubiously as Juice went inside of his own head. His head began to shake to match the grimace on his face. Jazzy-belle was a killer, not a thief. She had murdered many for the Family and never took a crumb from a victim that he knew of. "Our people don't steal!"

"Naw, that pretty, black mufucka don't steal!" Say-So nodded, agreed, and looked over to New York on the blanket with one of his female shooters. Joy was no Jazzy-belle but had plenty of bodies under her Gucci belt.

"Po-po prolly grabbed what they grab," Juice offered since the N.O.P.D was just as corrupt as the N.Y.P.D, L.A.P.D and many other police agencies around the country.

"Yeah," Say-So said but meant 'nah' since he was still looking at New York. He was the one who found the body, then called him before any police were notified. The work was gone by the time Say-So arrived which meant New York took it. The silent partner nodded in agreement with himself and moved on. "So, what ole girl 'talmbout?"

"Shit, let's get this money!" Juice cheered since he liked to make money. After all, he had sold his soul for money. "Enough to get your boys some basketball lessons..."

"Yeah, they suck," Say-So laughed as they looked over to the man stumbling and bumbling on the court. "That ain't the type of shooting I pay them 'fo tho."

"Shooters are good," Juice replied and looked over at his own. They were outnumbered and outgunned but would go all the way out at his command.

"I'ma need a sweet deal from ole girl," Say-So said so Juice countered with a number.

"Fifty/fifty. We'll supply the product. Leave it as it is, no more steps. None of that Fentanyl bull shit. Good, solid work and we split the proceeds." he offered since that was the offer. Any counter would be countered with gunfire.

"It's better when the dope is uniform," Say-So nodded. If all the dope was the same around town it prevented the migration of junkies in search of a killer bag. Not having to invest his own cash was a plus as well. The upside to dope was so high Big Mama could afford to supply him and still make a killing.

"So?" Juice offered and extended his hand. Say-So nodded

again and took his hand to seal the deal. The shooters on the court stopped shooting bricks when Juice stood. They stood down when Say-So shook his head. The mood was tense until the SUV was loaded and out of sight. Say-So looked at the picnickers and called, "Joy!"

"Mph girl!" New York grunted at Joy's ass when she stood from the blanket. He had spent the whole time together trying to talk his way into her panties. The thirty-year-old virgin liked pussy as much as he did so he was barking up the wrong tree.

"Sup?" Joy asked as she watched Juice's truck pull away. She was a little moist at the prospect of busting her gun but now they were getting away.

"Not yet..." Say-So said as he read her mind. It was just a matter of time until he crossed Big Mama and that required killing her men. In the meanwhile, he had something to hold her over. He looked over at New York just as a ray of sunshine made his new diamond pendant sparkle. "Nice chain."

"Tuh," Joy huffed and rolled her eyes. He talked about the new piece like it was the key to her vagina. It was nice, she just wasn't going to fuck him because he wore it.

"I think it's time to send ole New York back up to New York," he nodded and lifted the corner of her mouth in murderous mirth.

"Say less!" she cheered and happily skipped away. Say-So shook his head at her shaking ass as she departed.

CHAPTER ELEVEN

"I tole you!" Lil Baby boasted when Juice relayed news about the merger. Big Mama rolled her eyes and shook her head.

"Tell this lil girl how that ends," she directed. Juice scrunched his face at the request but the boss urged him on. "Go on nah!"

"It's finna be good, for a minute. Err body gonna make good money. The junkies finna be happy," he began, and Lil Baby began to smile and nod. Her grandmother smiled and nodded too since she knew the other foot was about to drop. "Then he gone try her. Soon as he figure he got enough money out us, he gonna try to kill your granny."

"Nuh-uh! We gone kill him first!" Lil Baby shot back at the thought of someone hurting her beloved grandmother. Big Mama was a little more ambivalent.

"Yeah, we gonna peep his network. His movements, people, trap houses," Big Mama relayed to the man tasked with carrying out her orders. "Then, we definitely finna kill his ass!"

"Where you going!" Lil Baby demanded when Bella emerged from the back.

"None yo bizness lil girl!" she shot back.

"My business tho," Big Mama added as Juice headed out. His work here was done so he was heading out to put it in motion. He grabbed Chad from the men's spot and left the premises.

"To the mall! School almost done. I need some summer clothes!" she insisted.

"Ion even like hearing the word, 'need'..." Big Mama grimaced. People died so her people's needs could be meant. Families were decimated by the drugs she sold so her family never needed anything.

"Well, want," Bella corrected. She was a lot of things but ungrateful was the least of them. Selfish, stubborn, and hot in the ass but she appreciated the life her grandmother provided.

"We're going to the mall," Buella announced as she came out next. There was a moment of silence as all eyes settled on the reclusive girl. Buella had rarely traveled beyond the bed and bathroom in the week since she had been back from the brink. Now she appeared looking like her old self even if a piece was missing. She was more stoic, and more determined than ever.

"Well, take lil bit with y'all," Big Mama advised and stood.

"We Ion even like this gurl!" Bella protested playfully.

"Y'all know y'all love me!" Lil Baby laughed and hugged her sisters. Buella halfway joined the hug, but something was missing. She left a piece of her soul back in the swamp house.

"I'm finna send Ray and the new boy to trail them." Ethyl sighed and pulled her phone. The call to the men's spot had them scrambling to pull out behind Buella.

Buella blinked at the spot where the bullet hole had been

before Big Mama replaced the windshield and head rest. There had been two other bullet holes she didn't see and never would since her grandmother had them fixed too.

"Hmp!" Bella hummed and smiled when she saw Cosby was one of the men assigned to watch over them. She pulled off the regular shorts she wore to get past her grandmother and revealed the tiny short below.

"Just nasty!" Lil Baby grimaced. She was nearly as thick as her middle sister who had closed the gap with the oldest one. But had no desire for people to see her ass cleavage bouncing from the bottom of the itty bitty shorts.

"Be careful," Buella spoke up. Both sisters snapped their heads in her direction since she rarely spoke.

"Huh?" Lil Baby asked from the back seat, but Bella knew she was speaking to her.

"Careful with what?" she asked and did the same thing that prompted the remark. She smiled at Cosby through the rearview mirror as they rode close behind.

"With that," she replied and continued driving. Anyone could see how smitten Chad was over the girl who was completely over him. Bella belonged to the streets and no one man would ever be able to tame her. Even the houseful of kids in her future wouldn't slow her down. No more than it slowed down their mother.

"Chile..." Bella laughed as Lil Baby looked back and forth between the two, trying to figure out what was going over her head. She wouldn't by the time they reached the mall, so she followed her sisters inside.

"Shit!" Cosby grunted as Bella's ass cheeks jiggled and jumped in the tiny shorts. He glanced over and saw Buella had just as much ass in the jogging pants doing a little juggling of its own. Lil Baby had on a pair of boy's basketball shorts but was all girl as well.

"Be very, very careful," Ray advised. He had taken in an eyeful of the asses himself but now scoured each direction for ops and threats. The safety of his own family was dependent upon the safety of these girls, so he took it seriously.

"I got a gurl at home. Kids and all," Cosby replied and shrugged. He saw Bella flirting, winking and smiling every chance she got but he was legit not interested. It was a nice ass though, so he admired it for the rest of the day.

The Fontenot sisters weren't the only nice asses in town though.

∼

"Damn you got a nice ass ma!" New York exclaimed as he walked behind Joy so he could admire that nice ass. "Word to my moms B!"

"G, thanks," Joy sighed and rolled her eyes. She had been through what the Fontenot sisters had been through at the hands of an older brother who viewed his little sister as live in pussy. She had been molested for years until she seduced a neighborhood killer into killing him in exchange for some pussy. She was a born-again virgin now because she said so.

Still, it wasn't the deviance that turned her off of men, it was the crassness. It was like dudes only saw her for what was in her pants and panties. Their relentless pursuit of pussy made her want some too. When she became a killer, herself it amazed her how men would follow her panty lines to their death. Just like New York was doing now that they entered the motel room. The ruse was Juice coming over so they could whack him, so they were both strapped.

"Shit, we may have a few minutes..." New York laughed and wiggled his brows to convey his meaning. She caught the hint, but he still hit her with a "Nawmean..."

"I do know what you mean," Joy nodded and looked at her watch. She lifted her shirt overhead and agreed, "We do have time."

"Dead ass ma!" New York exclaimed and snatched his pants off quicker than a New York Knickerbocker does his Velcro sweatpants. He lifted his shirt as she stepped out of her high heels.

"Can I wear your chain?" she asked when he was naked besides it. His clothes were folded neatly on the chair with his gun safely out of reach.

"Word is bond!" he eagerly agreed if it was going to get him some ass. He happily placed it over her head even though he planned to take it back the second the deed was done.

"Thank you..." she sang and removed her useless bra. Useless since her firm breasts didn't budge.

"Word up!" he smiled and marveled at the wonderful mounds of titty meat. He was so enthralled when he reached out and touched one he didn't notice her reaching behind her back until she came around with the pistol. "Huh?"

"Tuh," she replied and gut shot him. The bullet tore through his torso but didn't drop him.

"You bugging yo!" New York protested and took a step forward. The next shot to his knee would be his last and dropped him. "The fuck ma?"

"You stole B," she replied and mocked.

"Huh? Stole?" he asked, playing crazy like people will when under the gun. "I'm telling Say-So!"

"Who do you think told me to shoot you?" she laughed as he crawled for his phone on the table. Which just so happened to be right next to his gun.

Joy lifted her own gun to the back of his head in case he changed his mind and went for the gun instead. It crossed his mind, but he was pretty sure a bullet would cross his mind next if he did. He and Joy had put enough people in the dirt to know she enjoyed putting people in the dirt. He grabbed the phone and made the call. He put the call on speaker so she could hear the command to stand down.

"New York?" Say-So asked when he answered. He was surprised to see the name on the screen and asked, "Where are you calling from?"

"The motel B! This bitch Joy just shot me! Talmbout, I stole some shit!" He whined and waited for help. No help came since Say-So said nothing. Sometimes it's best to remain quiet and let people squirm. Squirm he did until he decided to try his luck with the truth. Or his version anyway. "You talking about the work at Pierre house? Nah, I got that out before po-po came! I still got that. Forgot I had it!"

"Sho nuff?" Say-So laughed. "Where's it at?"

"My crib! Oh wait, I sold a little bit, but I got the money," he laughed and grimaced at the same time. Getting out of this had him giddy but the bullets still stung.

"Get his keys and get that," Say-So ordered. "Keep it. Your tip."

"What about him..." Joy asked and adjusted the finger squeezing the trigger.

"He's fired," Say-So said so and she fired. The bullet plastered his next statement onto the wall. It would take a mind reader to read his thoughts off the wall.

"Thanks for the tip and chain," Joy said into the hole she just put in his head and pulled her clothes back on to leave.

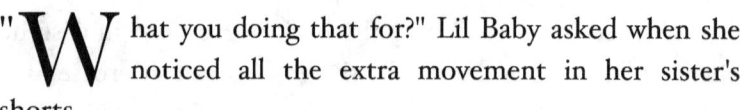

"What you doing that for?" Lil Baby asked when she noticed all the extra movement in her sister's shorts.

"Because she's trying to get that man into a fight," Buella replied for Bella and looked back. She expected to see Cosby glued to Bella's ass but found him looking back at her. She frowned her face up to show what she thought of being stared at.

"He must be gay," Bella decided and nodded. She was too pretty and had too much ass to be ignored so that was the only possible answer. She was getting plenty of attention from other guys so she started paying attention back. She collected phone numbers and clothes until it was time to go.

Going home required several more stops since Lil Baby needed beignets. Bella had to have crawdads and Buella wanted some ice cream. They were the safest girls in the city since the hitters watched their backs at every step. Well, Ray watched their backs while Cosby watched Buella's ass. His own woman was in for a treat since the pretty, yellow girl would be on his mind while he was up in her later that evening.

Buella caught him staring a few times and he would look away. The one time he didn't they engaged in a staring contest until she tapped out. He saw right through her, and she didn't like it one bit. Her name being called in the distance got louder until she felt a tap on her shoulder.

"Uh, Buella!" Lil Baby demanded and tapped again.

"What lil girl!" she fussed just like Lil Baby hoped she would. She may have been a boss in the making but was still a little sister. So, it was her duty to annoy her older siblings.

"When are you going back to school?" she asked.

"Monday," she answered quickly since she had already decided. She came too far to drop out now. Plus, her plans for college required a high school diploma. "Now, what about you lil girl? Don't end up stupid like..."

"Ooh, Look-it!" Bella shrieked and ran across a busy street

towards a shirt in a store window. Cars came to screeching halts and swerved not to run her down. Ray grimaced at the close call while Cosby went wide eyed. The near miss didn't miss Lil Baby though. She knew her big sister was stupid and didn't want to follow her footsteps even if the shoes were expensive.

"Grammaw says I have to go to school next semester anyway," Lil Baby sighed. Big Mama knew part of her plans for the girl required a formal education. Not just the reading, writing and arithmetic they taught but the social interactions as well. The girl needed to fight, reason, and resolve things on a smaller level before she could take over the city.

CHAPTER TWELVE

B uella didn't hear a word of what her sister was babbling
about as she drove to school for the first time in weeks.
It had actually been months since she had been in a heroin
haze for that long. Luckily, she laid enough of a solid founda-
tion all through school to be able to coast to graduation.

Sadly, she wasn't the only teen to get hooked on heroin in
her class. More of her peers were hooked on heroin than were
hooked on phonics. Of the hundreds of kids who started
ninth grade with her, a good half didn't make it this far. A
good chunk of the girls had a baby or babies to tend to. The
boys who fathered those babies didn't have any kids though
and added to another round of fatherless kids.

Likewise, a chunk of the boys opted out early and hit the
streets. Most sold a variety of drugs to the various drug
addicts. Drugs are a dirty business so a chunk of them realized the inevitables of the streets. They added to the inhabi-
tants of the prisons and graveyards around the city. So, her
bounce back was better than the fall offs of her peers.

"Huh?" Buella asked when she realized her sister was still talking.

"Bridget, she's pregnant again!" Bella said and shook her head. It was just a matter of time until she was back in the stirrups herself since she didn't use rubbers herself. She put a period between her and Chad but was already flirting heavily with a boy she met in the mall.

"Oh," Buella replied and tuned her back out until they reached the school. She pulled into the student parking and glanced back. She wondered what the security men would do while they were in class. Her answer came when Chad pulled into the parking lot and parked. They would sit right there until they came out and follow them back home.

"They don't make em like they used to huh?" Cosby remarked as he watched the grown children entering the schoolhouse. The girls were dressed like little prostitutes since they wanted to emulate the latest female rappers.

"Huh?" Chad barked but he heard him. He was so jealous of the pretty boy that he disagreed with whatever he said whether it was wrong or right, "Nah nigga."

"I know right," Cosby laughed since he found it amusing that Bella didn't want him anymore, but he didn't want her either. They slouched down and went their separate ways inside the car until class let out hours later.

"Principal DuPont wants to see you," Buella's homeroom teacher announced when she walked into the class-room. She was happy to see one of the students she was betting on looking like herself again. She nearly wrote her off with the others when she started nodding in class.

"Shit..." she grumbled and turned back around. Buella just

wanted to get through these last couple of weeks and cross the stage. She trudged up the hall and into the office.

"Hey girl, you good?" the secretary asked genuinely when she entered the office.

"Yes ma'am," Buella smiled back just as genuinely since she liked the woman. She was about to sit on the bench where students sat to wait their turn to see the principal, but the door opened.

"Hey gurl!" Bridget gushed when she saw Buella. Buella may not have cared much for her, but the girl had nothing but love for her.

"Hey, oh!" she replied and reeled when the girl hugged her.

"I'm glad to see you," Bridget announced with fresh semen on her breath.

"Miss Fontenot, come on in," Mr DuPont called from his desk. He was ready for a quick nap after his early morning blow job.

"See you later," Buella told Bridget since it was inevitable, for now. Her plans included never seeing her or this city again. She stepped inside as the principal let a deep yawn go. "Good morning Mr DuPont."

"Good morning to you! How you doing gal?" he demanded because he cared. He too had been betting on her since the ninth grade. Literally since the staff had a pool on which kids would make and which ones wouldn't. He already lost a nice piece of change when Bella didn't give birth before senior year. "Are you ok?"

"No. Not really," she revealed to even herself. She knew she was still a junkie even though she would never use again. She had the junkie gene and would have to replace it with something. God, music, work, or something.

"What can I do?" Mr DuPont asked and was ready to do it. Not just because he had money on her, he cared.

"You just did it," Buella smiled softly. His concern went a long way and gave her hope. She stood and headed back to class.

~

"Heads up..." Cosby announced when Bella stepped from the school between classes. Chad put his phone down and looked up as a giggling Bella hopped into a car with a basketball player.

"Fuck she going?" he wondered while Cosby had another question.

"Shit, how are we supposed to watch them both if they split up?" he wondered. Chad had a large lump of jealousy stuck in his craw so he couldn't speak. He coughed it up and decided.

"I can follow them while you stay here," he replied and started the car.

"Or, not," Cosby said when the couple climbed into the back seat. The next thing they saw was Bella's feet in the air. "Oh, that's gotta sting!"

"I'm finna go..." Chad began but Cosby held him back. "Fuck off me nigga!"

"My bad woadie," Cosby offered and raised his hands in surrender. "I'm just saying, the last thing we need is these girls telling Big Mama anything on us. I ain't tryna go wherever Buck went."

"Whatever nigga," Chad shot back but he knew the man was right. No one had the details, but everyone knew Buck's disappearance had something to do with them girls. He had no choice but to watch the car rock as the teen knocked Bella's boots in the back seat. Just like he used to do. His mind could hear her moans over her splashing pussy from where he was seated.

"High school..." Cosby laughed and thought back to his days in school. It hadn't been long, but a lot had changed.

Chad locked onto the smiling face when Bella and the boy stepped out of the car. He had been Thibodeaux's friend while he was alive. Then plotted to fuck his girl after he died. The ear-to-ear smile was because the pussy was just as good as Thibodeaux bragged it was.

"The fuck?" Houston said when a cold wind swept through him. He looked around but didn't see the evil glare glaring back.

"Come on," Bella huffed when she saw the source. She snarled and rolled her eyes at Chad and took Houston by the hand and led him back into the school. Cosby just shook his head. He knew then this couldn't end well, and he was right.

~

"Look bruh, we on the same team. The winning team," Cosby sighed as Buella appeared from the school after classes let out for the day. She waited near her vehicle for her sister to flirt and exchange numbers with more dudes. Houston told two friends about hitting Bella and they told two friends. Word spread and dudes flocked for the free pussy.

"Fuck you!" Chad grumbled under his breath. He knew they were indeed on the winning team but didn't like babysitting the brats. Especially having to watch Bella slinging pussy like a Frisbee.

SA'ID SALAAM

"Yeah, I know," Cosby laughed. Bella finally wrapped up for the day and came to the car.

"What?" Bella asked when she saw her sister's face all scrunched.

"You do know that err body tells err body else business in school, right?" Buella asked as an answer.

"Gurl! Do they!" Bella grunted and launched into the gossip she picked up for the day. "They say Bridget be sucking Mr DuPont thang err morning!"

"They also said you fucked Houston in his car during fifth period," Buella added as she pulled out of the parking lot. She sighed when she saw the familiar car pull out behind them.

"And he got a fat dick!" Bella laughed since there was no shame in her game. She went into graphic details from penetration to ejaculation, which her sister generally ignored. Except found herself fascinated today.

"Don't be leaking on my seats!" She fussed when Bella revealed she let him hit raw.

"I got tissue in my panties," she laughed. "I prolly need to get on the pill?"

"Or stop letting these boys come in you!" Buella stressed like she had so many times. She got ignored this time like the other times and her sister changed the subject.

"How 'bout Chad seen us?" she laughed as she locked eyes with her ex through the rearview mirror.

"Stop playing with that boy. Before you get him in trouble with Grammaw,". Buella warned. "These are dangerous people Bell."

"That nigga is the help. I helped myself to some dick. Helped him with some coochie. Ion owes him nothing!" Bella shot back.

"Chile you was just telling Big Mama y'all was in love a couple weeks ago!" Buella reminded and cracked up.

102

"Cuz, he made me come real hard," Bella admitted and joined her in laughter. Chad felt his blood boil at the thought of being laughed at. It was the kind of insult to injury that makes people do stupid shit.

"I got some runs to make," Chad announced when they neared the house. The girls pulled into the driveway, but he stopped in the street.

"Check," Cosby replied and got out of the car. He pulled off before he could even get the door closed.

Chad was mumbling and grumbling as he headed back the same way he came. Three quarters of the school parking lot had emptied since most students and staff went home for the day. Only the athletes, coaches and janitors remained. He slinked into his seat and sulked while the various teams did what they did in the gym, on the track and field.

"Hey...." a pretty cheerleader sang as she walked by the car. Chad snarled back and ran her off. He perked up when he saw who he was looking for and watched him walk to his car. The same car that rocked in unison with Bella's boots getting knocked.

Houston got some good pussy and had a good practice, which made today a good day. He was ready to eat some dinner, take a hot shower and rest up to do it all again tomorrow. His head nodded so hard to the music blaring from his system he didn't notice the car behind him turn every time he turned until he turned into his driveway.

Houston gathered his belongings to take inside the house while Chad got out and walked over. Houston finally registered him when he reached the driver's door. Having no enemies, he began a smile to greet whoever he was but Chad raised a pistol instead. The thirty round clip protruded from the handle the same way Bella's ass cheeks did in a pair of coochie cutter shorts. The modified clip in

103

the Glock turned the ordinarily wicked weapon especially vicious.

'Brrrrrrrrrrrrrrrrr' the nasty gun barked and sparked while Chad pointed it at where his face once was. The poor kid never knew what hit him or why. Chad wore a sinister smirk and headed back to his vehicle and pulled away.

What a day in the city of New Orleans.

CHAPTER THIRTEEN

"This chick..." Buella grumbled when she saw her sister's friend running up as she pulled into a parking spot.

"Gurl! Gurl! Gurl!" Bridget repeated before Bella could get out of the car.

"What, what, what, Dang!" she fussed. The mood in the parking lot was somber enough to tell whatever it was, was pretty bad.

"They killed Houston last night!" she gushed with an incongruent smile. The news was bad but being first to spread it still made her happy.

"Dang!" Bella reeled and shed a tear.

"They who?" Buella wondered and looked over at Chad and another man riding with him today. Chad's face was balled up even more than usual since Juice chose to let Cosby go with the rest of the crew on some real work. Even though he would have been upset had it been the other way around and Cosby had to babysit.

"They say it was the same folk that killed Thibodeaux!" Bridget reeled. That was just one of the rumors floating around over the senseless murder. According to some it had something to do with the basketball team.

"Hmp," Buella huffed and glared at Chad glaring back at her sister. He didn't see anything or anyone but her. A shiver ran through her spine and shook her head. "Ion ever want no one to love me like that."

"Who?" Bella asked and looked around. She did the opposite of Chad and looked at everyone except him.

"Buella crazy!" Bridget laughed as they headed inside. Once inside she peeled off and headed for the principal's office to get her breakfast in exchange for lunch money.

"Don't leave this building!" Buella fussed at her sister and regretted the words as soon as she heard them herself. For one it wasn't her job to tell the girl what to do. Plus, Bella didn't listen to her anyway. You can save people from everyone but themselves and Bella was going to do her, no matter what. "My bad, you can do whatever you want to do."

"You're right. I ain't going nowhere," she said somewhat subdued. Her big sister had changed right before her eyes, and it was almost as if she didn't know the girl. They both turned in different directions and headed to class.

Neither Fontenot girl learned much today since each was preoccupied with their own thoughts. Bella was concerned with clothes, lip gloss and fine boys. The latest music, movies and gossip was extremely important to her. More important than whatever her teachers were putting on the blackboard.

Meanwhile Buella was hundreds of miles away living her new life. The girl had everything in motion but wondered if she had the strength to pull it off. She knew New Orleans represented death and she wanted to live. She would love for her sisters to leave and live but had to accept they were too far gone.

Lil Baby was a little Big Mama by now. Everything about

her had changed as rapidly as her body did. The youngest Fontenot sister turned heads too when they went out but didn't seem to even notice. Part of Buella wanted to take her away with her but the life raft only had room for one.

"I'll come back and get you. On Gawd I will..." she pouted and turned the student's head next to her.

"Huh?" the boy asked.

"Ain't nobody talking to you!" she snapped and rolled her eyes. No one was as relieved to hear the bell ring as she was. "One more week to go..."

~

"**W**hat that thang talmbout..." Juice asked when the junkie returned from its mission. She was a person once upon a time until the drugs turned her into an inanimate object. The woman had a one-track mind that left track marks all up and down her once beautiful skin.

Her full lips once belted out the sweetest songs the ninth ward ever heard. She was Suge Avery to the rest of the choir, until the drugs got her. Now those same lips told lies and produced seeds from loins to lay, more tracks on her arm. The veins were now useless, like they were hiding from the dull needles she jabbed into them.

She was a regular on this side of town so she was tasked to buy some of the local product and bring it back. The men huddled in a motel room placing bets on if she would come back or not. Junkies are sorta like the ball on the roulette table. No one knows where they might fall.

"Looks different..." the woman said as she pulled her works and got to work. Cosby and Ray both blinked but didn't speak as she dumped the skag into the burned spoon. If either wondered how it got so black and burned the lighter, she produced from her pussy answered. She put the flame under the spoon until the dope inside began to bubble.

The woman pulled the same worn syringe and inhaled the drug up into the barrel. Cosby held his breath when she ran a finger up her jugular vein and found a spot. The skin resisted the dull tip but gave way under the pressure. She withdrew some blackish blood into the barrel with the dope before plunging both into her neck.

"Whoa..." Cosby heard himself say when he saw this part of the game. All eyes were on the junkie as her head began to droop where her breasts once were. The deflated bags of skin once nourished her children, but the dope took them away.

"Hmp?" Juice wondered since he wasn't sure. Word had gotten back that the dope on Say-So's side of town wasn't packing the same pow as it was a week ago. Part of the deal was not stepping on the dope. Both sides knew the fragile truce wouldn't last forever and this was the type of infraction Big Mama was waiting on. Then she could send Say-So with Pierre and have that part of the city to herself.

"It's a'ight..." the woman suddenly said as she suddenly came out of the nod. The weaker dope produced less of a high and required the junkies to use two and three times as much.

This caused a humanitarian crisis as Big Mama put it. She was right in an odd way since the junkies had to steal more shit and turn more tricks to stay high. That increased the crime rate all around. Not to mention if they ever stumbled across some good dope the increased dosage, they were accustomed to would kill them dead. Dead junkies were no good to no one.

"Well?" Ray asked to see what their next move was. Big Mama was ready to move but the call was on him.

"One shot, one kill," he decided. "Say-So and Joy gotta go but we can't miss. We don't need no back and forth..."

"I know where Joy stay," Cosby offered hopefully. Hoping to get the nod to permanently nod the dangerous woman.

"Ok, so go over there and dead the hoe," Ray chided and shook his head.

"I can, I will!" Cosby shot back more confidently than he should have been. He knew he was a pretty boy and pretty girls flocked like bees to nectar. Except he didn't have the kind of nectar she liked.

"Go over there and that bitch gonna send you back in a box!" Juice chuckled. "Nah, I know just how to get the bitch."

"What about New York?" Ray asked since the out of towner had a reputation of laying folks flat himself.

"They pulled him out the river last week," Juice replied and nodded at the internal struggle. Any time there was a rift in the crew there was room to wiggle in. His whole body did a wiggle when the plan came to mind. "One shot, one kill."

∼

"You're up Chad..." Ray announced when Buella stepped out of the house and headed for her vehicle. Rules were whenever one of the girls left the yard, they had a shooter on their bumper.

"Shit, I was supposed to, Juice want me to..." Chad hemmed and hawed since he only wanted to trail Bella in hopes of talking her into taking him back. He especially didn't want to leave her at home with the pretty boy around.

"I'm on her," Cosby sighed and rushed to his own whip before Buella could get away. If anything happened to her Big Mama would put a padlock on their hangout and set it on fire with them all inside. That dummy was willing to die about it, but he wasn't.

"Can't wait to leave here!" Buella shouted in frustration when she saw the car catching up to her. She went from poor and abused to rich and endangered when all she wanted to do was be regular.

Buella took unnecessary turns and ran stop signs just to spite the man on her tail. Her thoughts bounced around her head like a pinball until a wicked idea took root. She checked her rearview mirror before abruptly pulling into a parking lot.

"Shit!" Cosby fussed when he sailed past her since he couldn't stop. He knew she would give him the slip before he was able to find a spot to turn around. The fate of his woman and kid crossed his mind and he slammed on the brakes and made a dangerous u-turn.

He was just barreling up in the same parking lot when Buella stepped from the office. He pulled next to her car and watched as she used the key card, she just acquired to open the motel door. Buella looked back at him before stepping inside. Cosby stared at the cracked door for a few minutes before deciding to investigate.

"Hey dere..." Cosby called and tapped on the partially opened door, without looking inside.

"Come in," Buella called back from the bed. Cosby stepped forward and scrunched his handsome face in confusion when he saw her under the comforter up to her chin.

"What you got going on, Miss Buella?" he asked and looked around the otherwise empty room. She didn't have company inside, so he looked behind him to see if someone was pulling up.

"This..." she said and pushed the comforter away to reveal her nakedness beneath.

"Damn!" he exclaimed, wide eyed at the good, yellow

curves. Her plump breasts were capped with big brown nipples that were erect as he now was. His eyes dropped to the bushy box that hadn't been shaved since Sadie died.

"W,w,w,wa you got going on?" Cosby stuttered.

"I be seeing you looking at me. Well, here I am," she replied and spread her legs a little.

"I'm saying tho, what you want me to do?" Cosby whined since he didn't like this predicament one bit. Fucking the boss's granddaughter could get him killed. So could her telling Big Mama he tried to fuck her if he didn't comply.

"I want you to eat me," she moaned. Her box bubbled just hearing the words. Buella hadn't planned for anything beyond that but needed to bust a nut.

"Ok miss Buella," Cosby sighed and crawled between her thick, yellow thighs on his belly like a sniper. He reached up to part the soft afro covering her vagina, sending shivers through her soul.

"Arghh!" Buella grunted and nearly came just from his hand brushing against her box.

"Wow!" Cosby reeled. He was now fully invested when he saw her pussy blossom and swell like a rose in the morning sun. He leaned in and took a lick that sent more shivers up her spine. He locked his arms around her legs and clamped his thick lips on her box.

Buella bucked and moaned like a wild bronco trying to dislodge a cowboy from its back. He wasn't going anywhere though so she had no choice but to come on his tongue. Again, and again until she couldn't take it anymore.

"Stop!" she demanded, and he complied before she could finish the word. He wouldn't risk not complying so when she said, 'fuck me', he stood and removed his shirt.

Buella closed her eyes when he unbuckled her pants. That's how she got through the abuse she suffered through her childhood. Just close her eyes and mentally leave her body. She decided not to do that now. This was her choice, her consent. Her head shook a flashback away and she opened her eyes to watch him undress.

"Dang!" she marveled at his dick when it sprang free and quivered like a diving board after a dive. Cosby was too far gone himself now and climbed on top of the woman. Her legs spread as his tongue slid into her mouth. She winced from the mix of pain and pleasure as he eased inside of her. The men speculated that Buella was still a virgin since she had a girl-friend. Cosby confirmed that she was from the vicelike, vice tight box and grimaces and moans as he slowly stroked her.

"Shit," Cosby grunted when the volcanic vagina got the best of him. He paused his stroke to regain his composure but a contraction from Buella made him explode. "Shit!"

"Um, ok," Buella said when he stopped seizing from the strong orgasm. "I have to go."

"Ok," he agreed and gently withdrew. Buella locked onto his still erect dick, glistening in her juices and his come and changed her mind.

"One more time?" she asked hopefully.

"One more time," Cosby agreed and slid back inside of her. He fucked her a few more times but no one was counting.

CHAPTER FOURTEEN

"I think it's about time..." Say-So said as the bubble butt bounced in front of the table.

"Shole is," Joy agreed and rubbed herself through her jeans as reached out and touched the stripper's ass.

"That's not what I was 'talmbout, but I feel you," he laughed and let her have her fun.

"Mmhm," Joy hummed as her finger found what it was looking for. The dancer got slick and slippery but so did Joy as she rubbed one out right there on the spot. She came with a grunt and fell back in the booth.

"What you got a taste 'fo tonight girl?" Say-So dared. He and his right-hand woman often competed for pussy and she won more often than he.

"Strictly dickly!" the dancer answered even if she did just get fondled by the woman. They were both tipping, but she ascertained he was the boss and she preferred bosses even over dick.

"Ha!" Say-So laughed and stuck out his empty palm. Joy twisted her lips and filled it with hundreds. The boss laughed some more as he stood since her money was paying for his shot of pussy for the night.

"Whatever," she huffed and reminded. "We need to move on that old bitch."

"I just, never mind," he laughed off the subject he was trying to broach. "We'll talk about it in the morning!"

"Mmhm," she agreed and sighed as he left with the prize. Now she needed to find a snack of her own for the night. She looked up and scanned the club but doubled back to the jet-black beauty at the bar. She had been staring but turned away when Joy locked onto her. A moment later she was by her side. "Playing hard to get?"

"Ain't no play. I am hard to get," the woman replied but picked the diamond studded medallion from her cleavage for closer inspection. "Tuh..."

"Tuh hell, this piece cost more than some houses!" Joy said just like New York used to say when he used to wear it. Ironically, he bought it with the money he made from the drugs he stole from the man this chick killed.

"What's your name?" the nameless woman asked and scrutinized the rest of her. The designer labels added up to a tidy sum.

"Joy, cuz that's what I bring," she smiled to show off her new veneers.

"Dolly..." she lied in her reply since her real name rang bells. Jazzy-belle to be exact but they would have had to shoot it out right there on the spot had she revealed it. It would be easier, smarter and safer to get her alone, so she offered, "Wanna go be alone?"

"Only if I can ride these..." Joy dared and ran a manicured fingernail over her thick bottom lip.

"Sounds like a 69 to me," Jazzy-belle laughed and stood.

She tossed a few twenties on the bar and took the outstretched hand.

"We can get a room," Joy offered since she was too smart to bring strays home. This was a classy stray, but she still didn't bring strangers to her house.

"Already got one. I'm just in town for a job," she replied. Joy was no stud so she didn't open doors. She popped the locks with the key fob and they both climbed into the vehicle. She followed the turn-by-turn directions until they reached an upscale hotel in the French quarter.

"Nice..." Joy admired since it was better than the rat holes most of the hood rats she dealt with dwelled. "What kinda work do you do?"

"Corporate raider. Hostile takeovers mainly," she admitted as they stepped out for the valet. The upscale treatment rocked Joy to sleep so she left her gun behind. Besides, she never needed it to eat some pussy so she wouldn't need it tonight.

"Don't scratch my shit," Joy growled to the attendant as she passed off the keys. Jazzy-belle laughed since she knew she would never see the car again after tonight.

They turned heads as they walked hand in hand into the hotel. Jazzy-belle didn't mind the prying eyes or cameras since she looked different every other day. The long, blonde wig and designer shades hid her identity better than a ski mask.

"Nice!" Joy mentioned again as they entered the suite.

"You ain't seen nothing yet..." Jazzy-belle laughed and let her dress fall to the floor as she headed for the bedroom.

"Finna see..." she laughed and came out of her jeans as she hopped behind her. Jazzy-belle climbed on the bed and spread her luscious, black thighs to reveal the plump black box. Joy finished stripping and climbed on the bed with her. She positioned herself for the top spot in the 69 but Jazzy-belle had other ideas.

"Except, I on eat no pussy..." she admitted.

"Huh?" Joy asked since that's why they were here. She wanted to receive as she gave and turned around to investigate. The pistol with the attached silencer explained better than any words.

'PEW' the gun whispered and sent a slug that tore through her face.

The impact sent Joy flying off the bed, but Jazzy-belle was close behind. She tried to scream but the searing pain only allowed a high-pitched howl that only dogs could hear.

"Big Mama said Hey..." Jazzy-belle relayed and fired again. Joy fought, kicked, and rolled as the hired killer tried to kill her. She caught a few more rounds but none of the fatal wounds she was trying to deliver. The small gun clicked when the small clip was exhausted. She moved for her purse to retrieve the spare, but Joy had no intention of waiting. There was one shot, so she took it.

She summoned everything she had and hopped to her feet. She knew she wouldn't make it to the door when her killer slapped the fresh clip into the gun. Getting shot again was the lesser of two evils so she rolled out the window.

"Shit!" Jazzy-belle laughed at the choice. She rushed over to look at the splat but found Joy landed on the awning and rolled into the ground below.

She aimed but the screams and spectators began to murmur and look up to see where she came from. Jazzy-belle missed her mark for the first time. Now there was no choice but to run. She donned another wig and glasses before pulling on a different outfit. Moments later she passed the gawking crowd as she fled the scene.

"Ughh, Argh, Mmph!" Joy grunted to alert the crowd as

her would be killer walked by. She walked a few blocks to where she was parked and made the call before heading back up to Baton Rouge.

"Is it done?" Juice wanted to know when he took the call. Removing the shooter from the equation would make it easier to get to Say-So. Or just run him off completely.

"Naw, I missed," she moaned. "Don't worry tho, I'ma get her!"

"Missed? Bitch you just started a war!" He growled and hung up. He looked at the men looking back and conveyed the news. "It's guns up!"

～

"Gurl get out that window" Ethyl shrieked when Big Mama pulled the blinds open. She put her hands on her hips and looked out into the quiet night. The back-and-forth shootings had cleared the streets since the war began.

"This window prolly the safest place in the city rat nah," she sighed and looked down at her men posted out front. Her faith was more in technology than manpower though. That's why she didn't bat an eye when Lil Baby came and stood beside her.

"They coming," the teen remarked without a trace of fear. Meanwhile her sisters were hiding in the room hoping it would be over soon. There would be no more movement until it was. No school, no mall no walks to the store until the beef was over.

Graduation was a week away and Buella looked forward to what came after it. Cosby wondered what came next after their tryst but soon had his answer since Buella never looked his way again. She was so cold with it he began to question if it even happened.

Chad was busy shooting up any and every place Say-So had ever been. He was content to lay low until they shot up his granny's house. No one was hurt since Say-So was smart enough to evacuate his family, but the barrage of bullets knocked the old shotgun house completely to the ground. Then Pookie came and did what he does and reduced it to ash.

"Yeah, they is..." Big Mama agreed. Shooting at his people upped the ante and forced his hand. His own people would have abandoned him if he didn't clap back.

"Heads up..." Ray announced when a car came speeding up the block. It swerved from side to side and drew everyone's attention. Everyone but Big Mama, who knew that was too easy. Her head turned in the other direction and saw the slow rolling van approaching with the lights out. As expected, the car hit a corner and disappeared with the men all watching.

"Look now!" Big Mama shouted and pounded on the window to get their attention, but technology got in the way.

She was helpless when the van doors flew open, and shooters piled out. The synchronized shooters followed the plan and sprayed the guards out front. Two more took aim at the small house the men used as a headquarters and hang out. Meanwhile Say-So himself locked eyes with Big Mama and lifted the machine gun.

"Gotcha..." he smiled when the woman didn't move. Neither did the girl beside her but fuck her too. His smile widened when he pulled the trigger and sent a hundred rounds at her. The smile began to droop when the clip went empty, but the woman was still standing.

"Technology," Big Mama laughed when the bullet proof glass and panels did what she paid for and sent the rounds everywhere but inside.

"Let's roll!" Say-So shouted and hopped back into the van. The door to the house across the street began to open as the men piled back into the vehicle. They had mowed most of her men down but one stepped from the house as they pulled away.

Juice lifted the rocket launcher to his shoulder and took aim. He understood the blast radius and let them roll a hundred feet before he fired. The projectile entered the tinted back window and paused just enough for the men to register what happened. Two said 'oh' but neither reached the 'shit' before it exploded.

"Dang!" Lil Baby cheered and smiled at the carnage. The explosion turned the men into mush and set the vehicle on fire.

"Beefs over," Big Mama sighed and rubbed her grand-daughter's head.

"The city finna be ours!" Lil Baby sighed.

"Yeah, but first, get yo auntie off the floor!" Big Mama laughed at Ethyl, still flat on her belly.

"Ion trust no damn bullet proof windows!" she grunted as she got up. "Plus, beef ain't never over. There will always be someone coming for the crown."

"And they can have it," Big Mama reflected because she knew it was true. With one condition though, "Over my dead body!"

"Hmp!" Ethyl huffed since that's the way they got the crown.

CHAPTER FIFTEEN

"What you doing?" Lil Baby asked when she came into the room and found her sister putting items in a bag.

She may have been the only one in the house who noticed her slipping things out to her car every chance she got. Not all of her stuff, just the stuff most important to her. The gradual way a girl moves in with a guy, adding necessities along the way until half the closet is gone.

"Minding my business," Buella replied without a trace of sarcasm. This wasn't a catty moment but a teaching one, so she taught. "The world would be a better, safer place, if everyone minded their own business."

"Well, you is my business!"Lil Baby shot back. She wasn't being catty either and proved it with a hug.

"Eww, what y'all doing," Bella fussed when she walked in on the hug.

"Ewww what!" Buella demanded like she wanted some smoke. Lil Baby did too and came around to trap the girl. Once they had her surrounded, they attacked.

"Un-uh, y'all get off me!" Bella giggled and squirmed as her sisters hugged and kissed all over her face. The end of the war came as a relief to all, and moods were light.

"I got a run to make. Getting stuff for graduation," Buella sighed like it was a chore since her spoiled sisters didn't like chores.

"I gotta help Big Mama with the count," Lil Baby begged off. She really did have to count cash since her sharp eye caught shorts from the different spots. It seemed like the whore houses were always short, so she double checked their receipts by hand.

"I'm finna get some dick," Bella shrugged. Mainly because she loved to see her little sister grimace at the mention of sex. As long as she was disgusted, she wasn't fucking. Buella shook her head and laughed despite the memory of Cosby inside of her making her box jump.

"Be careful," Big Mama demanded when Buella passed through the living room.

"I am. I will, so I don't need no one following me!" she fussed and headed for the door. She stopped short, turned back, and went over to plant a kiss on her grandmother's cheek. She knew the woman loved her as best as she could. Even if she couldn't wait to get away from her and here.

"Ok baby," BigMama gushed and smiled at being loved on.

She hadn't rescinded the order of keeping an eye on the girls just yet since Joy was still out there somewhere. She checked herself out of the hospital days after surgery. The safe bet was she was in Houston or Atlanta since that's where people from New Orleans fled to escape natural disasters. Jazzy-belle was just that and was waiting for the one who got away to pop up so she could finish the job.

"I got it..." Cosby volunteered when Buella stepped out and headed for her truck. She hadn't looked his way since but

122

remained hopeful. Sometimes lighting strikes in the same place and that girl had a bolt of lighting in her panties. It was hands down the best pussy he had thus far. Thinking he deflowered her only added to it.

"I don't need no one following me!" Buella shouted but directed it to Juice. Juice happened to look up and saw Big Mama give the nod that let her go. She still kept watch in her rearview to make sure she wasn't followed. Her plan required secrecy and she got it.

"Can you take me to the mall?" Bella asked as a formality since Big Mama had loosened the reigns.

"I'm finna make a run. Ask one of the guys to run you," she replied while Lil Baby twisted her lips at her since she just told her they were going out. "Have Chad run you,"

"Anyone but him!" she rolled her eyes and headed out.

"These gals today!" Ethyl added and shook her head.

"Same as we was when we was young!" Big Mama reminded since they used to run through their share of men and boys when they were teens. "This lil one gonna be breaking hearts!"

"Who! Ewww!" Lil Baby grimaced and fussed just like the women hoped she would. Because again, as long as she was disgusted, she wasn't fucking. Boys were still yucky to her and that was just fine. Especially since the girls up the street she fought were all already fucking. Luckily Lil Baby's scratch faded away, so she let it go.

"Big Mama said one of y'all need to run me to the mall!" Bella demanded as she stepped to the men's new spot.

"I got..." was as far as Chad got before she shut him down.

"Anyone but him," she fussed without even looking his way.

"Run her..." Juice ordered Cosby even though he was no longer the lowest man on the totem pole. New faces replaced the dead faces, but Juice was still selective about who he let around the girls. Just being at the main house was a step up from the other task around town.

"Me?" Cosby asked even though the man was looking right at him. Which was why the man just twisted his lips as a reply. "Come on!"

"Don't nobody want you!" Bella huffed and winced when they got into the car.

"Good, so we even," he shot back and pulled out of the driveway.

He happened to glance at the thick, yellow thigh on the passenger seat but ignored it. He heard rumors of her and knew she dealt with Chad which turned him off, not on. He personally never understood how dudes all lined up to deal with the same chick. It was like running a slow-motion train and turned his face up at the thought.

"Ion know who you 'posed to be, turning your nose up at me!" Bella fussed as she read the thoughts written on his face. "I'll tell my granny and..."

"Tell your granny what? That I don't try to holla at you?" He laughed and mashed the gas a little more. The sooner he got her there the sooner he could get her home. Bella was fuming at the rejection, but it was the laughter that made her blood boil. It's said hell hath no fury like a scorned woman, but a spoiled teen is a close second.

Almost as close as Chad was on his bumper since he followed them the whole way.

~

"Dang!" Bella admired her sister in her cap and gown. "Sometimes I don't think I'ma ever make it!"

"Hmp," Buella huffed playfully then quickly remembered

this was no time for play. "Yes, you will! Next year and then you can do whatever you want in life! You're smart, you're pretty and you are worthy!"

"You just made it weird," Bella fussed and left the room as Lil Baby entered.

"Dang!" she proclaimed as well.

"Thanks," Buella said and pulled the garment off. She would put it back on once they got to the graduation. Today was the big day and she could hardly believe she made it.

"Come on chile! Don't be late for your own graduation!" Big Mama called from the front. Buella didn't want to be late, so she grabbed her cap and gown before looking around to make sure she didn't leave anything she planned to take with her.

"Love your hair girl!" Ethyl gushed. The simple braids ran straight back to her lower back but framed her face like a museum piece.

"Thank you!" Buella smiled.

"You got your outfit for tonight?" Big Mama asked but didn't leave room for an answer. "We got a big weekend planned! Shindig tonight, BBQ tomorrow..."

"Yay," Buella offered but Lil Baby squinted at the incongruity on her face. The ladies didn't notice but they weren't raised by Buella either though. Something didn't quite add up, but her math was a little rusty from the year off from school.

"Well, let's skedaddle..." Big Mama announced and picked up her purse.

"I'ma ride with Buella!" Lil Baby decided.

"No!" Buella shrieked with enough force to stop time and turn heads. She realized they didn't know what she knew and quickly fixed it. "I'm trying meditate on the big day,"

"Mmhm," Big Mama agreed since she couldn't exactly

disagree. Her grand babies were three levels of weird, so she shrugged her shoulders and continued.

Lil Baby wore a snarl as she climbed into the back seat of the SUV with her grandmother. Juice closed their doors and let Ethyl into the passenger seat before coming around to get behind the wheel. Buella felt the eyes on her and turned her head to meet Cosby's gaze.

She almost felt bad for the cold shoulder she gave him after giving him some good, hot pussy. He was ready for an eye roll but instead she cracked half a smile for him. He would have to get the other half in the next lifetime since she turned away and pulled off.

"Driver..." Bella summoned like a boss and stood beside Cosby's car. He let out a sigh and let her in but wished Chad could get her back so he could get out of the middle of whatever they had going on. Which was actually nothing since the fickle young girl had moved on. Chad and another man pulled out behind them, and the convoy rolled over to the high school.

The graduation was being held on the track and field the Fontenot sisters rarely used. Buella was more academic and Bella just hella prissy to be running and sweating on the field. The family filed into the rows of seats while Buella donned her cap and gown to join the other graduates on the stage.

"A'ight nah, don't y'all cut the fool. Shake my hand with one hand, get your diploma with the other!" Mr DuPont began in his normal pomp for the circumstance. He softened for a second and added "I'm proud of y'all. I really am!"

"Thank you Mr DuPont!" they all replied but Buella a little louder. He had been a rare constant in her haphazard, hectic life. They shared a nod that conveyed her appreciation and his acknowledgement before he took his place to begin.

"Hey gurl!" Bridget huffed, out of breath, as she slid into the seat behind Buella.

"Huh?" Buella wondered. Bridget had on a cap and gown too which made no sense to her since she barely went to class and was dumb as dirt to prove it.

"I ain't suck all that dick 'fo nothing!" She shot back louder than necessary but had a point. Plus, she didn't have anything on under the gown since Mr DuPont planned to take her home after the ceremony. At least she was smart enough to get a diploma with the dick.

Buella was elsewhere as her classmates stood and crossed the stage. Most complied with the instructions not to cut the fool, but some couldn't help themselves. A few danced, others ditty bopped, and Bridget had to twerk just a little.

"That's you..." the girl beside Buella said and gave her a nudge. For all the listening to names she still managed to drift inside her own head before hers was called.

"That's my baby!" Big Mama proclaimed and whooped and hollered when Buella stood. Her sisters beamed and clapped as she collected a hard earned, battle-worn diploma.

"Thank you," she repeated to Mr DuPont with tears streaming down her face. He nodded and the next name was called.

The ceremony continued until all names were called. A few got blank pieces of paper since they still had a few credits to make up over the summer. The caps sailed into the air as the crowd erupted in cheers. Buella made sure to only toss her cap a few feet so she could catch it. The families smiled for pictures while the kids mingled one last time since most would never see each other again.

"I'm so proud of you girl!" Big Mama gushed with a rare tear falling from her eye. She handed Buella a thick envelope when she released her from the hug.

"Thank you," Buella smiled broadly. She knew the envelope was stuffed with cash and she knew just what to do with it.

"Let's ride over to the restaurant now and get our eat on!" Big Mama declared.

"I'll meet y'all there," Buella said and headed for the student parking lot. She could see the SUV pull out and turn left towards downtown as she inched along out of the packed lot. She was relieved the security stayed on her grandmother, so she turned right and went in the other direction.

Buella spent as much time in the rearview mirror as she did looking at the road in front of her. No one was following her, so she made the first stop of her mission. She rushed inside Sadie's old apartment and collected her things. The things she purchased and kept there as well as the things she moved from Big Mama's house. They were all by the door in preparation for today.

The SUV was quickly crowded but she managed to get it all inside. One last trip and she looked down at the gun kept with the money. A moment of contemplation ended in a head nod, so she grabbed the pistol too and rushed down to the vehicle.

Now Buella didn't look back as she sped along until she pulled onto I-10 E to I-65 N. It would take her to I-85 North which would take her to her destination. Meanwhile, her family was waiting back at the restaurant.

"Where the heck is this girl?" Ethyl grunted when her stomach growled. They were waiting on the guest of honor before they ordered but an hour had passed.

"Hmp!" Big Mama huffed, flushed with intuition. She processed the girl's demeanor lately along with what she had been through. She knew she returned from the swamp with a different girl than she took out there. Her head nodded when she stirred in what she had gone through with her own daughter. "Y'all go 'head and order."

"We not waiting for Buella?" Lil Baby asked.

"Nah chile, she not coming," Big Mama replied. She doubted she would ever see the girl again. Not in this life anyway.

CHAPTER SIXTEEN

"I can't believe she left us," Lil Baby pouted as she looked at Buella's vacated bed.

"Man, fuck that girl!" Bella snapped. "She is selfish! Always been selfish! Don't care about nobody but her damn self!"

Lil Baby twisted her lips but didn't say a word. Bella was actually the most selfish human being she ever met. The world revolved around her as far as she knew. Plus, Lil Baby was old enough to understand the sacrifices their older sister made for them. She understood she used herself to divert their devious daddy's attention.

"That's messed up," the youngest moaned and accepted that her sister was gone. Life would have to go on, so she knocked the tear away and deleted Buella's number from her phone. It was symbolic mainly since she knew the number backwards and forward from memory. Her calls had been going straight to voicemail anyway since Buella turned her phone off.

"I'm 'outa here!" Bella decided and stood. Big mama knew

they were hurting so she didn't question her as she traipsed through the living room and out the door.

"You up," Juice said when Bella stepped out of the house. Big Mama had a run to make so one of the guys would have to take her where she needed to go.

"Sheesh," Cosby groaned and shook his head. He really disliked the spoiled brat even more lately. She had turned up the shade and disrespect after being laughed at. Still, he understood the power she held and held his tongue. He managed a smile and opened the door to an SUV. "Afternoon."

"Tuh," Bella scorned and rolled her eyes. Cosby turned his head, so he didn't see up the short skirt as she climbed up into the vehicle. He saw Chad glaring back at him to make sure he didn't. Which caused him to look and get an eyeful of luscious, yellow ass cheeks protruding from the French cut panties. He turned back to Chad and bit his lip while grimacing.

"I'll drive slow so you can keep up," he chuckled at him as he came around to the driver's side and pulled off.

"This boy..." Juice sighed when Chad hopped into his personal vehicle and followed like he did every day. Not that he minded the extra security on the girl but this situation between the two shooters would eventually end in shots. His thoughts were interrupted when the door opened, and Big Mama stepped out.

"I'm finna have a car delivered. Put this bow on the top when it come," she advised and handed him a big, red bow. It would go on the red BMW she had purchased for Bella a little while back. It was some consolation for her older sister leaving.

The car would definitely appease the material girl, but Lil Baby was fit to be tied. Her face had been balled up since the graduation. Big Mama would never admit how hurt she was. Especially since Buella fled pretty much the same way her Beatrice had flown the coop.

Both were similar in the fact that they were drowning on dry land. The pressure and expectations of being related to Big Mama was overwhelming at times. Definitely not for the faint of heart that is but Bella and Lil Baby loved it. The power to move men was powerful and intoxicating.

The car arrived shortly later, and the men gathered around as Juice put the bow on top. No one was surprised when Lil Baby popped out. They all turned their heads so they didn't see how fine she got. Fine enough to make Buck vanish and no one wants to vanish.

"Ooooh! This is pretty!" she gushed and rubbed her hands over the car just like Bella did when she first saw it.

"Watch this..." Juice announced and hit the key fob. He was all smiles as the hardtop began to open and fold itself into the trunk.

"Oooh!" the girl cheered and bounced causing the men to turn away again. Some just went back inside to be on the safe side.

"Hmp!" Ethyl huffed at all the bouncing and jiggling Lil Baby was doing without trying.

"Child don't even know how fine she got," Big Mama laughed. Lil Baby wasn't much into fashion but dressed more like Buella in the athletic gear since she didn't want to dress like a hoochie like Bella.

∽

"I need to shave my legs..." Bella suggested and put her legs up on the dash as they rode up the road. Cosby pursed his lips and lifted his head not to look as he drove.

Bella got a kick of making him uncomfortable every chance she got. Knowing it made Chad mad was just icing on the cake. She looked in the mirror and saw him looking right at her. A smile spread on her face when he got caught by a red light and couldn't cross the busy intersection. It spread even more as she spread her legs and turned up the pressure.

"What the hell are you doing..." Cosby fussed when she lifted up enough to shimmy out of her panties.

"Finna make myself cum," she said and tossed her panties at his face.

"Chill girl!" he grunted and swatted the undergarment aside. He wanted to hold the dainty panty up to his nose and inhale the sweet melody of a fresh, clean vagina but didn't. He did look in the rearview and noticed he lost the tail for a moment. He made a few unnecessary turns to add to the distance just to fuck with him.

"Dang..." Bella grunted when a flutter floated through her body. She had just been playing but began to writhe from her own touch. Cosby blinked in disbelief when she bust a nut all over her fingers. "Whew! I need some dick now! Take me to my friend's house..."

"Nah, I'ma take you somewhere and fuck you myself!" he declared and pulled off. He reached over and slid a finger inside her as he drove.

"I thought, ssss, you ain't like me..." Bella moaned and gripped his wrist while working her hips. She clamped her tight box around his finger and bust another nut.

"Shit!" he proclaimed and stomped on the gas pedal. He managed to reach the same motel he bedded her sister in and secured a room. He intended to put her through the same course once they got inside.

"Oooh!" Bella reeled and giggled when he tossed her onto the bed. Then leaned up to watch the handsome specimen get naked. He even kicked his socks off, but Bella was practically naked even when she was fully dressed. She pulled the dress overhead and her panties were back in the vehicle. A loud hiss escaped her throat when he leaned in and licked her swollen vagina.

Bella was far more experienced than her estranged sister. She gripped his head and tossed her legs far and wide. It wasn't long until she bust another nut in his mouth. Cosby ran his tongue from her box up her torso and plunged it into her mouth. At the same time lined the dick up and plunged in with a splash.

"Fuck!" Cosby sighed when he got inside of her. It suddenly made sense to him why Chad was so obsessed with her. His mind flashed to his own woman at home as he contemplated leaving her. Her loving moans only intensified the heat and pressure.

"Fuck," he repeated when a quick nut came bubbling up. He snatched out and bust on her stomach while she leaned up to watch.

"Dang!" Bella giggled but didn't have a chance to laugh long.

"Shit!" Cosby shouted when the door burst open behind him. He made a move for his gun but didn't make it.

'Brrr', Chad's gun barked as it sent several rounds his way. Two of the three rounds peeled the top of his head off and slumped him over.

"Owe! You shot me!" Bella groaned from the wayward third round that missed its mark and tore into her torso.

"Shit! I'm sorry baby!" Chad panicked as he came out of the blind rage that made him kick in two other doors before finding the right room. "It's ok baby! I'm finna take you to the hospital!"

"You shot me mother fucker! My granny is gonna kill you!"

she shouted and clutched her stomach. "Big Mama gone kill you dead!"

"Yeah..." Chad sighed and stopped in his tracks. He had fucked up and Big Mama was definitely going to kill him. There was only one thing left to do so he raised the gun and did it.

'Brrr...'

~

"Where the hell is this girl?" Big Mama fussed when the grandfather clock chimed midnight. "She finna turn into a pumpkin..."

"Hmp," Ethyl grunted knowingly since she knew she left with that hunk of Cosby. She knew exactly what she would be doing with him, and how. "Boy got back shots written all over his face."

"Ride that face, backwards..." Big Mama laughed at how she would ride a fine, young stallion like that. She suddenly recalled she hadn't had a boy toy since her last one got eaten by an alligator.

Meanwhile Lil Baby looked back and forth between the two older women and wondered what they were talking about. The soft knock on the door turned all heads. First to the door, then over to the clock. It was definitely midnight so Big Mama pulled the small pistol she kept tucked in the tuft of her chair and stood.

"Come on," she called since whoever was knocking had to get through a whole lot of shooters to knock.

"Hey um Big Mama. We uh, got a problem," Juice offered solemnly. His head lowered so he wouldn't have to see what could come but had already called his wife just in case.

"My baby," she managed as all the wind escaped her chest.

136

Her knees buckled causing her to back peddle but Lil Baby popped up to prop her up.

"What happened!" Ethyl demanded as she came to her feet as well. Juice shook his head at even having to say the words. They had to be said so he said them.

"Her and Cosby were, um, found in a hotel room. They uh, someone shot them," he managed.

"Are they dead? Is my grand baby dead!" Big Mama roared similar to how a fire breathing dragon breathes fire.

"Yes ma'am, I'm sorry. They gone," he sighed and lifted his head to take his medicine. He was head of security, and this happened on his watch. An infraction that warranted the death penalty and he understood that.

"Where is she?" Big Mama asked. This wasn't the time to mourn. Even Lil Baby looked and blinked as she processed the unbelievable turn of events.

"Down to the morgue. They need you to come identify the um, her," he managed. She reached for his arm, and he led her out of the house.

"Stay here baby," she told Lil Baby over her shoulder. She may as well told it to the magnolia tree because her granddaughter never broke stride. She closed the back door before Big Mama got settled in the passenger seat. Ethyl slid in beside Lil Baby for the silent ride down to the morgue.

Big Mama lost count of how many times she had been here, to do this. She even came here to identify Clarence after killing him herself. She recalled the neat little hole she put in his forehead from a similar two shot Dillinger like the one in her purse. That one was in the swamp since she was too clean to hold onto a dirty gun.

"You have a Bella Fontenot?" Ethyl asked as they made it inside.

"From over on," Juice added since the body was still a Jane

Doe until formally identified. Cosby had identification but his wife was still on her way to make it official.

"I'm her grandmother," Big Mama managed.

"Yes but..." the clerk replied and searched for words. "It's um, bad."

"I'll do it," Lil Baby offered when she saw her grandmother shudder. The determined look on her face won Big Mama over. Plus, for her to one day take her place she would need to see things like this for herself. Plus, she had done a lot of shit but this was one thing she couldn't do.

"Ok," she agreed, and Ethyl escorted her to the chairs.

"This way..." the clerk announced and took her into the rear. The smell of antiseptic and death mingled in an odd mixture that crinkled Lil Baby's face. The incongruent aromas clashed like corduroy and silk. They stopped short before opening the door for another warning. "It's bad."

"You said that" the teen replied stoically and pushed the door open.

The clerk remembered exactly which drawer contained the teen even though there were several more teens in the room. In fact, they saw more and more teens as society continued to deteriorate. She pulled it open and stood back. She braced herself for the outburst that never came.

"Dang Bella," Lil Baby sighed when she saw what was left of her sister's pretty face. She didn't even register the hole in her belly.

The 'switch' installed in Chad's Glock turned it into a fully automatic machine pistol. A quick tug on the trigger sent a short burst of rounds that literally removed Bella's face. Lil Baby just stared, didn't blink, and absorbed it along with all the other filth she waddled in on a daily basis.

"She wouldn't have felt a thing," the clerk lied. The gut shot wouldn't have come after the six to the face.

She couldn't know how long Bella writhed in pain from the belly wound but knew she did. The door opened and another clerk escorted another grieving family member inside. They used to process one at a time, but the soaring murder rate made them churn and burn to make room. Literally since the thirty percent who went unclaimed were quickly incinerated in the crematorium.

"He's over here and I have to warn you, it's not pretty," the clerk warned as she slid the drawer open. "Oh my!" the woman grunted and grabbed the drawer for support. Cosby was missing the top of his head beyond his eyebrows.

His brain had actually fallen out when he was put inside the bag. It was currently in the fridge where one clerk hid his lunch so the other clerks wouldn't steal it. "That's what you get, Cosby! messing with some bitch!"

"Cosby? Bitch?" Lil Baby asked and looked over. She registered the pale face of the dead help, then his pretty girlfriend who just called her sister a bitch. There was nothing to talk about now, so she attacked.

"Shit!" one clerk shouted and ran from the room when Lil Baby ran over and swung on the woman. The unexpected blow rocked her, but she stayed on her feet and fought back.

"They're fighting!" the clerk shouted when she reached the waiting room.

"Lawd..."Big Mama sighed and led the charge towards the back. They entered the room where Lil Baby and Cosby's woman were engaged in battle. Juice moved to break it up, but she spoke up first. "Nuh-uh, let 'em chunk."

And chunk they did since Cosby's woman was a grown woman. She came up in these same streets and had a nice pair of hands herself. She gave as good as she got, and they were both lumped and bloody. Lil Baby would have fought to the death, but her opponent had kids at home.

"I ain't mean to call yo people no bad name!" she huffed and puffed in search of a breath.

"Say sorry then!" Lil Baby shouted with what little wind she had left.

"I'm sorry," the woman relented, and both finally let their guard down. She recognized Juice and asked, "Who did this to them?"

"I don't know yet," he admitted even though he had a pretty good idea since Chad hadn't returned. He made a round of unauthorized collections from a few of the trap houses and got in the wind. "Fixin to find out tho..."

The woman nodded at an unspoken threat, then turned to give Lil Baby a nod as well. Both signed the papers to claim their dearly departed.

CHAPTER SEVENTEEN

"I swear I ain't in the mood for this bitch!" Big Mama snarled when they returned to the house and saw detective Larue sitting in her car.

"I got her..." Lil Baby said and hopped out while the truck was still moving.

"Come back here girl!" Big Mama called after her. The last thing she needed was her last grand kid catching a case for assault on a peace officer. "Go in the house!"

"I'm sorry for your loss Eleanor," the detective offered sincerely. She paused for a reply, but Big Mama just glared. "Look, let the police handle it. He's going to prison. Where I'm sure he will be dealt with."

"You talking like you know who did it?" Big Mama dared. She knew too and put a hundred grand bounty for the killer to be brought to her alive.

"I'm only telling you this since it's fixing to be on the news," the detective disclaimed and continued. "Motel cameras recorded one Chadwick Tillman pull up and kick in several doors before shooting your grand baby. Ballistics matched another murder a few weeks back. Killed a student in his driveway. He's not going to wiggle out. Let us handle it. Then, when he gets to Parchman, do what you do."

"Ion do nothing," she declared and marched back into her house.

"They didn't get him, did they?" Ethyl moaned. This could only end one way for there to be any justice and satisfaction.

"No but they on him," she replied and looked at Juice. "Let's make a run."

"Come on," he agreed. Their men were scouring the city, but she couldn't just sit in the house.

"I'm coming," Lil Baby announced and followed out of the house. The teen hadn't shed a tear just yet but the bow on top of the car her sister would never drive pushed one from her eye. Just one and she quickly knocked it away. She wanted to be mad, not sad so tears would have to wait.

The city moved at the speed of New Orleans at night. Junkies, dealers, and thugs roamed the hood. Crickets sang along with the sirens and gunshots to add a soundtrack to the warm night. Lil Baby hadn't been out at night since they left the ninth ward. There they could sit outside and watch the hood drama in real time. Now she was a part of it.

"Here we go Big Mama," Juice announced when the boss hadn't realized they came to a stop.

She nodded and pulled her own door open to step out. Her granddaughter was close behind as they made their way to the front door. She only got one foot on the front step when the door began to open. Juice stepped up and upped his gun but didn't fire.

"I heard about what happened! I'm so sorry!" Myrtle moaned and pushed the door open further as an invitation.

"Is he here?" Juice asked as he pushed inside first. He went from room to room with his gun but Big Mama didn't wait for him to clear the house.

"He's not here," Chad's grandmother answered to Big Mama as she and Lil Baby stepped inside.

"You ain't heard from him?" She dared and focused on facial expression, inflection and stutter like a human lie detector.

"No ma'am," Myrtle vowed.

"What about his mama?" she asked since she didn't live here.

"Died a few months back. Found her with a needle still stuck in her arm," she replied. It didn't register to Big Mama that it was probably her dope that killed the woman. But then again, her dope killed lots of folks and she didn't care about any of them either.

"Where else y'all got people?" she asked to determine where to look next. Chad was a sucker for love but still smart enough not to stay in the city.

"Houston, Atlanta..." she shrugged and named the spots many fled to after Katrina and never returned. Most just added to the crime rates of other places.

"Hmp..." Big Mama huffed and looked around. She picked up family pictures and flipped them over to read the words on the back. Lil Baby studied the two women and saw when Myrtle flinched but said nothing. "Well ok den."

"I'm so sorry about your grand baby," she offered again before they departed.

"I know," Big Mama sighed and spread her arms. Myrtle came over and embraced her for a second. She didn't see the straight razor in her hand, but Lil Baby did. Her eyes went wide when her grandmother made a quick swipe that made the woman clutch her own throat.

Myrtle stumbled away as she contradicted herself by

choking herself while trying to save herself. Blood squirted from between her fingers in her futile attempt to keep it inside of her neck. Each beat of her heart sent a fresh rush between her fingers.

The woman locked eyes as the killed asked her killer why with pleading eyes. Big Mama twisted her lips since she should know. She raised the piece of shit who killed her granddaughter is why. Myrtle didn't have enough blood to stand so she sat. She kept squeezing but the blood kept squirting. With less velocity with every beat of her heart. Until it slowed to a trickle, and she fell over.

Lil Baby stared into the lifeless eyes and wondered what they could see. The gaping hole in the woman's neck showed just how proficient her granny was with that razor. The cut ran from ear to ear, severing both jugulars as well as her trachea. It was a wonder the woman lasted as long as she did.

"Call Pookie over here," someone said. Both Big Mama and Juice turned to see it came from Lil Baby.

"Yes ma'am," Juice replied after a nod from his boss. He made the call that would burn the house and headed back to their house.

"What next?" Juice asked since he knew more blood had to spill. Maybe his own and he was ok with it. As long as his granny didn't die clutching her throat.

"Gonna get some rest," Big Mama said wearily. It was late so the road trip would wait until morning.

"Where we headed..." Lil Baby finally announced after the city was an hour and a half behind them. Big Mama rolled her head to look out the window instead of answering. The girl sighed but left it alone. Her answer came just over an hour later when they exited at the sign for Simmesport, Louisiana.

Juice glanced back to make sure the small convoy was still behind them. He didn't think they were needed since Chad was just one man. Plus, he knew Big Mama planned to pull the trigger on this one herself.

She had her personal forty caliber Glock in her purse, but had it modified with the same type of switch as Chad had in his. It was only right after all since an eye for an eye requires equal wounds. The Lord showed who was boss and cast a beautiful sunset no artist or AI could rival. Because no matter how pretty they made it, it was still a replica of what HE actually created.

The approaching night cast covered the operation that would start here but wasn't meant to end here. Big Mama had called ahead to set things in motion, so the men just formed a perimeter. She sent a text and got one back that gave the nod.

"Thank you auntie Lionetta!" Chad cheered when his aunt placed a plate of her gumbo in front of him at her table.

"You welcome chile," she sang and watched that first bite. A good cook knows that the first bite says all that needs to be said about their cooking.

"Mph! Mmhm!" Chad hummed and nodded as chewed. He was so busy chewing and swallowing he didn't notice the movement around him. First his aunt slid the bag he kept on him every second away from his feet. She carried it with her and opened the door for the company. "This good auntie!"

"Glad you enjoyed it," she sang and stepped aside so her company could enter.

"My grand baby ate a hot pocket as her last meal," Big Mama announced once she was inside. Chad recognized the voice without looking and went for his gun. Big Mama held the bag containing the weapon that murdered her people. "Looking for this?"

"Auntie?" Chad pleaded with the hurt of being set up evident in his voice.

"You killed a child!" Lionetta shot back and shook her head. Big Mama saw her in the picture at Myrtle's house and called ahead. Killing the girl was part of it but the bag containing the hundred-thousand-dollar bounty sealed his fate.

"It was an accident!" he told his auntie then quickly realized he should be explaining to Bella's people. "It was an accident! I shot Cosby, but she got hit!"

"So why you ain't take her for help?" Big Mama had to ask. The coroner said she could have survived the gut shot had she got help. Instead, he sprayed her face with nine millimeter rounds.

"Cuz, I know you was gone kill me," he pouted. If pouting could help it would have because it was a really good pout. It wouldn't though so Big Mama gave the nod. Chad tried to fight Juice and the other man but neither intended to let him win. They beat him down and tied him up.

"What about her..." Juice asked and nodded towards Lionetta. They never left live witnesses because dead witnesses can't testify. You can ask them whatever you want but they won't answer.

"She's good," Big Mama said and looked at the bag in their host's hand. It was stuffed with cash that she earned by providing the justice she deserved. The women nodded thanks and welcomes before she turned to leave.

" You with them," Juice told the man after they loaded Chad into the trunk. "Y'all can go on back to the city."

"Ok," he replied and picked one of the vehicles containing

the rest of the men. They headed back to New Orleans, but Big Mama had a stop to make along the way.

Lil Baby recognized her surroundings when they reached New Iberia. The smell of the swamp confirmed it before they turned down the dirt road that led to the house. The land creatures scurried away from the approaching car. The thumping and bumping in the trunk intensified when they came to a stop. Chad must have sensed this was the end of the road. He was right too since this road ended in the swamp.

"Aaaargh!" Chad shouted ferociously when the trunk popped. Juice just twisted his lips since a shout ain't never solve nothing.

"Come on out of there," he ordered and pulled his arm. Chad tried to resist until the man switched the switch that flipped his knife open. He had seen Juice poke enough people with that knife to not want to get poked.

"Come on with it then!" He decided and stop resisting. Juice helped him out of the trunk and into the house where the women were waiting.

"Aaaaah!" Lil Baby screamed and attacked. Her fist and feet pummeled the man but didn't do much damage. She beat him for several minutes until her fist bled and she ran out of breath. That didn't stop her from biting a chunk out of his cheek and scratching his face with her short fingernails.

"That's not what we here for baby..." Big Mama said as she slid the sliding door open. She hit the flood light as Juice came over with the bag, he picked up from the supermarket before they left New Orleans. The whole chickens inside weren't safe for human consumption since they hadn't been kept below temperature. The gators didn't seem to mind though and scrambled for the appetizer.

"Hmp?" Big Mama wondered when Ole George didn't

show up and clear them away. What she didn't know was his run of the swamp was over when a new bull came of age and size.

Lil Baby looked back and forth between the condemned and the swamp. Getting eaten alive by alligators was poetic but wouldn't give her satisfaction. She held out her hand and locked eyes with her grandmother.

"She was my sister!" She reminded when Big Mama began to shake her head. She saw the steely determination in her eyes and handed her the weapon.

"Buck was right. You is the finest one out of all y'all," Chad laughed as she approached with the gun. He laughed but the irony was it was Buck who taught her how to handle a gun, even though she never fired one.

"Mmhm," she replied and pressed the gun to his forehead.

'Brrrr,' the gun spit as it destroyed his face and head. He tilted over in death but that didn't stop the girl. Lil Baby pointed down and pulled the trigger again.

'Brrrr, brrrr, brrrr,' the gun spit into his head until there wasn't much head left. The last rounds tore into his body until it clicked empty.

"Gimme another one..." Lil Baby asked as she popped the clip out like Buck had taught her.

"I ain't bring another," her grandmother replied almost apologetically. Lil Baby blinked, then turned to Juice.

"Here," he sighed and handed over his gun. She quickly emptied into Chad's empty shell as empty shells littered the floor. Most wildlife scatters at the sounds of gunfire but the gators knew it was the dinner bell.

The gun clicked empty, and Lil Baby reached for another. Juice looked at Big Mama who shrugged her approval. He gave it to her, and she knew exactly how to load it. She hit the lever to cause the slide to chamber a round and quickly unloaded it too.

"That's enough," Big Mama intervened when she reached for another. Juice got another nod that pressed him forward. He drug the bloody mess of what was left of Chad to the edge and pushed him into the water.

The body barely got to splash before the gators rushed forward and pulled off pieces. The murky water churned and bubbled as the alligators spun and twisted to devour the meal. They began to scatter when the new bull approached. He grabbed the lion's share and sank to the bottom of the swamp to enjoy his meal.

"He needs a name?" Big Mama announced. The quiet room went quieter until Lil Baby spoke up.

"Bella," she decided, and the swamp had a new king. The satisfaction only lasted until they reached the car. Lil Baby blinked in the reality that she was suddenly on her own.

CHAPTER EIGHTEEN

"Man!" Buella exclaimed and did a slow twirl to take in her surroundings. The small, one bedroom apartment was tastefully furnished with secondhand furniture from a thrift shop but it was hers. Her drug money was more than enough to pay the year lease in advance.

She had plenty of cash between what she squirreled away from her generous grandmother. Then what her girlfriend gave her and finally her own hustle. Her clothes stuffed the small, walk-in closet and she had everything she needed to start her new life in Atlanta.

"Huh?" Buella asked when she heard her sister calling her. It made no sense since she hadn't turned her old phone back on from the day she got here. No one had the number to the new phone so she didn't know where Lil Baby's voice just came from. She realized it was in her head, so she gave it a shake to dislodge it.

It was pure curiosity that made her pull the old phone out and turn it on. It buzzed for several minutes from the text, emails, notifications, and voicemails. Buella knew it could only be bad news since back home was nothing but bad memories. She decided to just turn it off but her pretty little sister's face popped on the screen along with her number. It took strength to press the button to take the call.

"Hello?" Buella asked even though that's not a question. She figured her sister had a lot of questions since she left without saying goodbye.

"Ion know why you don't call me back! I told you it's an emergency!" Lil Baby whined into the voicemail again as she had been doing for the last couple of days. The funeral was tomorrow so she called and left messages every few minutes.

"This is me," she intervened when she realized her sister thought she reached the recording again.

"Buella? This you?" she asked happily. She was so excited to hear her big sister's voice she momentarily forgot the grim news she was calling to bare.

"Yeah, it's me. How you doing?" she asked and looked around her apartment again.

"Fucked up is how I'm doing! Bella is dead!" she revealed and heard Buella gasp.

"Don't play with me girl!" Buella demanded. "Dead? How? What happened!"

"Chad killed her! He kilt her and Cosby in a hotel room! They say he killed some boy in ninth ward too!" she reported as Buella fell to her sofa.

"Told that girl to stop playing with him! I told her!" Buella fussed and moaned. Hot tears flooded her mouth as she wailed. "Big Mama's going to get his ass!"

"I got him!" Lil Baby proudly proclaimed even though she knew better than to speak over the phone. Buella didn't process the statement since she couldn't imagine her Lil Baby killing someone.

"Did y'all have her funeral? You know she loved her pink!" Buella asked.

"It's tomorrow. We got pink everything. You have to come!" she pleaded.

"I know!" Buella replied. She knew she had to go just as well as she knew she wasn't. "I love you, Agatha!"

"I love you too! See you tomorrow!" Lil Baby smiled and rushed to convey the news. Her grandmother was pulling on a menthol and sipping on her brandy when she came rushing into the room.

"What's wrong chile?" Big Mama asked even though this was the first smile she had seen in the house since the murder. Murders, since the girl was now a killer herself. Big Mama wondered how it would affect her, but she asked for beignets on the way home. Then slept like a baby when they got home.

"I just spoke to my sister!" she shot back causing the women to shoot glances at each other. Both wondered if she meant her dead sister since Buella's phone had been off since she left town. "Buella, say she coming tomorrow!"

"Oh, ok," Big Mama sighed. She waited until she departed the room before pushing the words from her mind into the universe. "That child ain't coming."

"Nah, she not," Ethyl agreed. They both knew how much it takes to leave this city. Which was why they never did, and never would.

"**W**here the hell is she!" Lil Baby barked when Buella's phone went to voicemail the next day.

"Tuh!" Big Mama snorted in response. She wasn't sure if she would be more shocked if the girl showed or didn't show. After all, she did see the girl piss and shit herself in the throes of withdrawal. Her shoulders involuntarily shrugged since she long ago chose her status and money over family.

In Buella's defense she tried to come. She packed a bag, filled her vehicle with fuel but just couldn't do it. She made it to the entrance to the highway but just couldn't do it. She ended up at the zoo because she had never been to the zoo before in her life.

"I'm never gonna forgive her if she doesn't come," the teen snarled and stomped out of the house. The red car with the red bow stopped her in her tracks. She remembered when Bella came home gushing about the car. Now she would never know she actually got it.

"Y'all ready?" Big Mama asked when she stepped out of the house. The crew certainly looked ready since everyone was dressed in Bella's favorite pink.

"Yes ma'am," Juice sighed and adjusted his pink tie. He opened the door for her and let her inside. Lil Baby didn't wait for him to open hers. Which was probably good since wearing a dress was foreign to her by now. She climbed in, wide legged giving the world a view of her pink panties under the pink dress. No one would have looked anyway but it was still better.

Big Mama spent big to send her granddaughter off in style. The streets were lined in pink balloons the entire route to the church. It too was decked out in pink flowers and balloons. A blown-up picture of Bella pretty in pink smiled next to the pink casket. A closed casket since Bella was a mess inside the box.

"Baby!" Bridget moaned and spanned into Lil Baby when she entered the church. She squeezed the wind out of her right in the doorway. "I can't believe she gone!"

"Me either," Lil Baby sighed. She nodded at her pink outfit when they separated then headed for the front pew.

Lil Baby didn't register a word of what the pastor was babbling about but that was for the best. The man never met the girl in the box so his words would have just pissed her off. Instead, she paid attention every time the door opened. Big Mama did too but wasn't expecting her granddaughter. They were both disappointed each time another latecomer came in, other than the one they were pining to see. It if were a race Big Mama would have won.

"Who is that?" Lil Baby asked when a brown skin bombshell walked in, wearing a lacy pink dress. Pink heels added six inches to her curvy frame and the pink feather on the pink hat added another few inches. The pink veil obstructed her face, but Big Mama didn't need to see through it to know who was behind it.

"That's your auntie," she announced and tried to stifle a smile. Beef or no beef she was happy to see her daughter.

"Beatrice?" Lil Baby asked since she barely remembered seeing the woman. Seeing her now made her heart flutter since she had that effect when she walked into a room. Big Mama usually looked twenty-five years younger than her actual age. Now her lookalike daughter aged her in an instant.

Every head and eye watched the regal woman walk up the aisle to the front pew. Even the pastor stuttered when he saw her strut all that stuff. Mounds of luscious, brown titty meat heaved from the dip in the pink dress.

"Hey Big mama," she greeted as she slid next to her mother. She offered a hand and Big Mama accepted it.

The church part of the service wrapped up and they headed out to the pink limos to take them to the graveyard. Big Mama paid for the limos and Hearst to be wrapped in pink for the day. Beatrice climbed into a black Bentley and joined the procession.

Lil Baby finally lost it when her sister's casket was lowered into the ground. The finality fell on top of her like a ton of bricks and made her take a knee. Big Mama was too consumed with her own grief, so her aunt dropped to a knee too, in the pink, silk stockings that cost a pretty penny.

"I'm sorry. I loved your sister. Sisters..." she corrected and looked around for the missing face.

"Buella ain't come! I hate her!" Lil Baby growled. Being mad felt better than being sad so she allowed it to take over.

"No! Don't you say that girl! You..." Beatrice began but saw her mother in her mouth. This was a conversation for another time so she would wait for that time. She helped her up to finish sending Bella off. "Go give your sister her flowers."

"Yes ma'am," she sighed and headed over to drop the pink bouquet down the hole, onto the pink casket. Big Mama slid beside her daughter for a word.

"You look nice," Big Mama began since she installed vanity in the girl while still in diapers.

"Where's Charles?" Beatrice asked instead of acknowledging the compliment. She knew she looked nice since she always looked nice. Right now, she wanted to know where her brother was. His plot in the ground was empty and that was the only reason she could think of for him to miss this. She knew Malva was on drugs and wasn't surprised not to see her.

"He's not around anymore," Big Mama replied and lifted her chin. Beatrice blinked in disbelief until she believed it. She had no doubt her mother would kill him or her since she was who she was.

"The mama too?" she asked since Malva wasn't around. Junkie or not she could still see her child off.

"Over there," she nodded with her head. Beatrice followed her eyes to a row of graves and nodded. "How long are you in town for?"

"Couple days," Beatrice replied. "Can I take my niece shopping?"

"Come to the house. Let's talk..." Big Mama answered and walked off. She collected Lil Baby and headed back to the limo.

CHAPTER NINETEEN

"Whew! I swear, if there's one thang I miss about home..." Beatrice grunted and leaned back to unbutton the top button of her jeans. She had swung by her hotel after the burial to change into a pair of skin tight jeans. A bowl of Big Mama's crawdad etouffee made them that much tighter.

"Hmp," Big Mama huffed despite the compliment. Ethyl shot her a glance but held her tongue. This was family business unrelated to The Family business so she would mind her business.

"So, how you doing in school Agatha?" the visitor asked her niece. The girl was snaggle tooth the last time she saw her but was now blooming into full woman hood.

"Fine," Lil Baby replied even though she hadn't been to school in a year. Which of course was just fine by her.

"That's good baby. Get good grades and you can be anything you want to be," Beatrice counseled as a good auntie should.

"Tuh," Big Mama grunted again. Lil Baby furrowed her

brow at the obvious tension between the two women. Maybe because they looked so much alike but more probably because they thought so much alike.

"We can go for a walk if you want?" Beatrice offered so they could get it off their chest without loading it onto the young girl's back.

"Like we used to," Big Mama replied with something that almost looked like a smile. Except smiles have merriment while this showed malice. They slid their chairs back and stood like one person. Lil Baby looked back and forth between the two as they headed out. Two of the men moved to follow but Big Mama shut them down. "No!"

"I reckon shouldn't no one wanna kill you in yo own neighborhood..." Beatrice offered. It sounded a little more sarcastic than she meant it but was out, so she left it.

"Hmp," she huffed as they walked. The men still followed from a distance just in case.

"Say what's on your mind mama," she dared. It must have been the opening Big Mama was waiting on since she jumped in with both feet.

"Saw one of your movies..." she put out like the cheese on a mousetrap.

"Which one? I got what, twenty-five?" she asked even though she was quite sure. She was Big Mama's only daughter, so she was on top of her business.

"Ion know the name, but you was sucking a dick," her mother replied.

"Well, I suck dick in all my movies," Beatrice happily reported since she knew the woman didn't like it. Oddly she didn't mind selling heroin but sucking dick on film was a no-no. "Unless I'm eating pussy."

"It was a white boy. With a big ole, curve dick. Look like a boomerang," Big Mama managed to get out with a straight face. Not for long though.

"A boomerang? Really mama!" Beatrice cackled and cracked up. Big Mama had a hearty laugh as well even though hearing her child call her 'mama' tugged at her heart strings.

"Why you doing that girl? You so pretty! So smart!" Big Mama asked and added the compliments to soothe the questions she always wanted to ask. Her initial reaction was shame, then anger. Now she was just confused.

"You really want to know?" Beatrice stopped and dared.

"I, you, because..." the woman stammered through different angles of blame. Until the finger of blame landed on her like a game of spin the bottle. A heavy sigh pushed the answer of her own question from her mouth. "Cus of Clarence..."

"Yup. Ding, ding, ding..." Beatrice sang but there was no prize for this correct answer. The closet door was open, so she let all the bones fall out. "He used to fuck me so much I started to like it. Not being molested of course, just sex. I would let boys do the same thang and I liked it.

Clarence taught me how to suck dick, so I sucked dick in the hood. Them boys taped me doing it and that shit spread so fast and far I couldn't go anywhere in the city without being recognized. After graduation I loaded up my car and drove west. Damn near drove into the ocean tryna escape the shame.

Then I ran out of money so I did a movie. It went crazy so I used my head for more than just giving head and branded myself. I own my movies, my brand, my website. My name, image and likeness earns me thirty grand a month and I ain't made a movie in years. I got stocks, bonds and..."

Beatrice's speech was interrupted when her mother snatched her into a hug that pushed the wind from her lungs.

She caught so off guard she thought the woman attacked her for a split second. Until she heard the sobs and felt the warm tears on her neck.

"I'm sorry baby!" Big Mama moaned. If she had a dollar for each time she uttered those words she wouldn't be able to buy shit. Because she was never sorry, until now. The brash woman charged hard and unapologetically through life, her whole life.

"That's what I been waiting to hear my whole life!" Beatrice moaned and mingled her tears with her mother's. What took a lifetime to break was healed in a few minutes. The mother and daughter returned hand in hand with exact matching smiles. The sad irony was it took death to bring them together.

~

"This is nice!" Lil Baby exclaimed when she buckled the seatbelt in the Bentley.

"Thanks, but it's a rental. I got a white one back home," Beatrice replied and started the vehicle with the press of a button. She twisted her lips when one of the cars pulled out behind them. She stressed to her mother that she didn't want security men following her, but Big Mama sent them anyway.

"Secret service. Grammaw the president!" Lil Baby laughed and watched the car behind them. She locked eyes with Jernika and the pack of girls on the block. They rarely left the block since school was out and Lil Baby was rarely out.

"You know how to drive Agatha?" her auntie asked.

"I'm sure I could," she replied. She learned everything else by watching so she was pretty sure she could. She was about to find out when Beatrice pulled over.

"Uh-oh..." Vance proclaimed when the car glided to a stop.

"Uh-oh!" one of Jernika's friends said too when the car stopped.

"Ion got no problem with that gurl!" she protested since she didn't want to fight her again. She lost that fight and had to whoop all her friend's asses again to keep her spot. Except Lil Baby never looked their way as she changed places with her aunt and got behind the wheel.

"Fuck we 'sposed to do nah?" Vance asked since he couldn't protect them from getting into an accident.

"Ion know," the other man shrugged as the Bentley pulled away.

"Ok then! Look at you!" Beatrice cheered when her niece expertly maneuvered the four hundred-thousand-dollar vehicle. She pulled up to the valet when they arrived at the mall and got out.

"Now, let's go shopping!" Beatrice announced. She didn't have any kids of her own to spoil. She used to buy stuff for Buella and Bella when they were little and before she moved out of town.

"Ok," Lil Baby shrugged since she wasn't a shopaholic like her sisters.

"I'm tryna figure out your style..." Beatrice wondered and checked the girl out. She wasn't sporty like Buella and had no interest in being sexy like Bella. She fell somewhere in the middle, so she racked up on the entire C-money clothing line.

Each member of the iconic girl group Pretty Thugs had their own clothing line that was as different as their individual personalities. Z-money's line was sexy, P-money's was slutty and C-money was more conservative since she understood the power of influence.

The VIP service shuttled bags of clothes and shoes to the

vehicle and the duo hit the food court for lunch. Beatrice turned heads with each step and finally someone stepped to her.

"I loved you in your last movie!" a well-proportioned, well-appointed man greeted. The security men quickly flanked him, but she waved them off.

"Thank you, even though it's old now," she smiled. Beatrice semi regretted the career that made her wealthy and always made sure to put it in the past tense. "You look familiar too..."

"I play for the Saints," he explained while the security men nodded. Star running back or not they would have flipped him before he could touch her.

"I love basketball!" Beatrice gushed, causing her niece to squint.

"That's football auntie!" Lil Baby corrected and shook her head.

"Oh, ok! Well, I love football too!" she sang and twisted one of her curls coyly. Lil Baby squinted curiously since she wasn't the same woman, she had been a moment ago.

"Well, let me invite you to a game," he said and pulled his phone. She pulled hers too and he sent her his info. "You call me if you get hungry."

"I'ma be hungry later," Beatrice replied while her niece soaked in all in. She had nothing to do with it now but had it.

"Then call me later," he smiled and walked off.

"See how that's done?" Beatrice asked.

"Uh, yeah?" Lil Baby replied and laughed.

"You have a boyfriend?" her auntie wondered. She noticed boys noticing the girl since they arrived, but Lil Baby didn't seem to notice or care. Her still walk belayed the curve of her spreading hips and roundness of ass.

"Ewww! No!" Lil Baby grimaced. Beatrice just blinked and

processed. She was old enough to like boys so something unnatural had to disrupt the balance. Her mind shot back to when Charles would do to her what Clarence did to them both. She wouldn't ask but her head nodded to her conclusion.

"Come on, let's get some shoes!" Beatrice cheered. "You like Manolo Blahnik?"

"Ice cream?" her niece wondered. She wouldn't know a Coach bag from a stagecoach, but didn't care. Not yet anyway. Ice cream did sound good though so after lunch they found a spot and sat down to catch up.

"You know what I do for a living?" Beatrice asked once they settled at a table.

"Un-uh," Lil Baby replied too quickly but it was the flash of shame that gave her away. Her auntie twisted her lips into a 'yeah, right' so she came clean. "Yeah. I heard grammaw talk about it. She cried. Said it was her fault."

"Hmp," Beatrice huffed just like Big Mama does. She thought about it for a moment and sighed. "It's our fault."

She accepted the trauma was on her mama but how she handled it was her bag to carry. The sad reality is more women and girls are sexually abused than aren't. Very few move on to become porn stars so she wouldn't, couldn't put it on her mother. No more than anyone can someone for how a trauma affects them.

"It ain't how you start, it's how you finish!" Beatrice declared. She saw the confusion on her niece's face and spent the rest of the afternoon explaining.

Lil Baby was a sponge, and this was just more to soak up.

CHAPTER TWENTY

"Mmmmmm-muh!" Big Mama grunted as she hugged and kissed Beatrice at the airport. The two could pass for sisters with the matching ear to ear grins. It's amazing how many times intense beef can be settled with a simple 'I'm sorry'.

"You guys gotta come out to Cali and visit!" Beatrice insisted.

"Yes!" Lil Baby bounced and clapped at the prospect. Thus far she had only traveled beyond her city on a couple of occasions. Neither was exactly a vacation, so she was all for it.

"Mmhm," Big Mama hummed and shook her daughter's head.

"Mama, 'Nawleans ain't finna blow away if you leave for a lil while!" she laughed.

"Ion know, it might!" her mother joined the laugh, but Lil Baby knew the woman well enough to know the laughter didn't go past her mouth. She really did think the city would blow away without her foot on it.

"Love you..." Beatrice practically dared and braced herself.

She hadn't heard it from her in so long she wondered if she would hear it now.

"Love you too baby," the woman replied and got another hug. Lil Baby squeezed in and got her some too before the gate closed. Beatrice turned and ran onto her flight and headed home. "Welp..."

"Welp," Lil Baby repeated as they headed out of the airport to go home.

The house seemed emptier than ever before since Buella and Bella left. Lil Baby rejected the thought of remodeling to make it a one-person room. Instead, she would alternate sleeping in her sister's beds. Both had left new and nearly new clothes behind.

It had been years since Lil Baby played 'dress up' but couldn't help trying on their clothes and imitating them in their mirror. It was all fun and games, but she was just as sexy as Bella in the tiny skirts and tight shirts. And just as rugged as Buella in her sweat suits.

She checked her phone everyday looking for a message, missed call, text or DM from Buella, but they never came. Each rejection made her heart a degree colder towards her sister. So cold that it soon resembled hatred.

Meanwhile Buella was still crying her eyes out weeks after the funeral. She missed her sisters as much as Lil Baby did. If not more since she helped raise them. The brutality of Bella's death only confirmed her resolve to never return.

Buella barely escaped with her life and had to take two lives to do it. She would always be 'that gurl who kilt them gurls' as long as she was in New Orleans. In Atlanta she was just another pretty face in a city of pretty faces.

In New Orleans she could only be, 'Big Mama 'ndem folk', with enemies and security everywhere she went. The weight of that nearly caused her to hunch from the pressure. Here she could walk upright and bask in obscurity.

Buella had a nice cache of cash but still found a job in a record store. It kept her busy enough for summer to fly by in a flash. Soon it was time to start classes for freshman year of college. She wasn't the only one starting a new school.

∽

"You ready girl!" Ethyl called down the hall.

"Tuh!" Lil Baby huffed in reply. It was the first day of high school and she had no intention of going. Especially since she was enrolled in the school on this side of town instead of the one back in the ninth ward where she grew up. Bridget would still be there along with Suzette and the rest of her associates from the neighborhood. Now she had no friends or associates in this neighborhood.

"Come on nah, don't be late on your first day!" Ethyl pleaded. Big Mama just twisted her lips and rolled her eyes. She said what she said, and the girl was going to school. She was going to get a diploma, but more important was the social interaction. The teen acted more like a forty-year-old woman than a teen.

"I ain't finna be late," Lil Baby grumbled but her reflection in the mirror made her smile. She fit nicely in one of Buella's sweat suits and rocked one of Bella's designer T-shirts. The expensive tennis shoes on her feet capped off her first day outfit.

Big Mama braided her hair into two long braids that hung to the middle of her back. It was amazing that the same hands that shed so much blood could make a perfectly straight part. The braids could be used against her in a fight, so she evened the score with a straight razor like her granny carries.

"Want some breakfast?" Big Mama asked when she finally emerged.

"Or coffee?" Ethyl snickered since the girl was so grown.

"No, no," she replied with her lip pulled into a snarl and marched out of the house.

"She cute tho," Big Mama added and smiled. They finished their coffee and Ethyl stood to leave. Big Mama was right behind her since she had to make her rounds alone.

"Huh?" both women asked when they stepped out and didn't see Lil Baby in the SUV. They did see the car cover used to cover Bella's BMW. It was on the spot where the car had been parked but the car was gone.

"I sent Vance after her," Juice offered.

"Why you ain't stop her!" Big Mama fussed and headed for her car.

"Stop Lil Baby?" he asked, wide eyed with wonder. She couldn't stop the girl from doing anything so how in the world did she expect him to.

"You know what..." the boss asked, and everyone paused to find out what this what was. They would have to figure it out on their own because she hopped into her vehicle and pulled away.

"Guess I'll um, shit, um..." Ethyl stammered. She couldn't figure it out and just walked back inside.

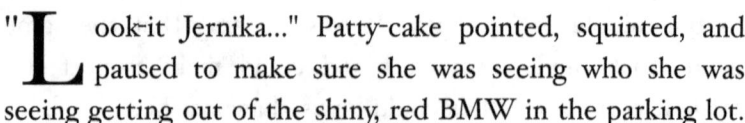

"Look-it Jernika..." Patty-cake pointed, squinted, and paused to make sure she was seeing who she was seeing getting out of the shiny, red BMW in the parking lot.

Her head nodded when she was sure, but still asked, "Ain't that the girl from up the street?"

"Shole is!" Jernika confirmed and began to march in her direction. She adjusted the scrunchy on her tiny ponytail as she approached.

"Come on with it..." Lil Baby growled when she saw the pack of girls stepping her way. She expected to have to fight so the sooner the better. Hopefully she would get suspended so she could go home. She quickly tied her braids and tucked them in her shirt and put her hands up.

"Ion want no smoke..." Jernika surrendered on arrival.

"Well, what you want then?" Lil Baby wanted to know, and explained, "Cuz ain't nothing but smoke over chere!"

"Good cuz you finna need it. These hoes finna try you!" Jernika advised while the others nodded in agreement.

"Shole is!" Patty-cake nodded vigorously as she took in how pretty the girl was. She was pretty herself with smooth, chocolate skin and a thick crop of her tucked under a wig like the rest of the girls. Someone made wearing wigs cool so the high school was filled with a bunch of girls looking like little bank robbers.

"And?" Lil Baby needed to know since she knew that much as well. Big Mama did too and sent her anyway. Part of being sociable is whooping some asses. These were the people she would have to deal with in the city as adults, so it was important to make alliances along with the inevitable enemies.

"And you stay in our hood!" Patty-cake partially explained and turned to Jernika for the rest.

"So, you with us! We the Hot Gurls!" she cheered happily. Having the pretty girl with the mean fight game was a plus.

"Hmp..." Lil Baby huffed and wondered. She knew Big

Mama had allies since you needed them. Her head nodded with understanding then suddenly stopped. "I'm good."

"You really not," Puddin offered. "We ain't jump you but these hoes definitely finna."

Lil Baby looked around and saw the eyes looking back. Some locked in because the face was new. Others because of the car. The boys saw the booty and the girls noticed the clothes. They were right and she knew it but still held her ground. Big Mama taught her that whoever brings the deal to someone else is in the weaker position to negotiate. Kinda like being on the bottom in a 69, but she didn't quite understand that analogy.

"One condition," she offered since she was in the top. She had their full attention and continued. "I'm the leader!"

"Nuh-uh! I'm the leader!" Jernika shot back.

"She whooped your butt tho," Patty-cake reminded. Having the girl with the hands and a car was a plus for them all.

"It ain't about that!" Lil Baby quickly corrected. Jernika was an asset because she could fight so she wouldn't alienate her. She even leaned in to hear what it was about. "If we are a crew then we need to rock together. Eat lunch together. You finna pay for us?"

"Lunch is free!" Jernika shot back in defense of being broke.

"I ain't finna eat that!" Lil Baby grimaced and the other girls did too. The school lunch wasn't bad, but it wasn't good either. It was food though and some of their houses didn't have food.

"You finna pay for all our lunch?" Choo-choo asked wide eyed and gave a quick count. Well, not so quick since math wasn't her strong point. She was fine though and got her nickname for letting guys run trains on her. "Six of us?"

"Unless Jernika finna pay?" she wondered and joined all eyes on her.

"I ain't got no money!" She reeled and relented since she wanted to eat too. "I mean, I guess. But I'm second in command. Vice president!"

"Nah, she is," Lil Baby said and nodded towards Patty-cake. She knew Jernika would lose any vote, so it was what it was.

"Well, I want a muffaletta for lunch then!" she bargained from the bottom spot.

"Deal..." Lil Baby agreed and ushered in a new era for the Hot gurls.

CHAPTER TWENTY-ONE

"Mmhm..." Big Mama hummed and tilted her head when Lil Baby arrived home from her first day of school.

"I ain't wreck!" she offered as an excuse for taking the car without permission.

"You ain't got no license either chile," the woman fussed. Not that she minded her breaking rules since she was teaching her to do just that. "Juice finna get you some fake ones but you need to take the test and get some real ones!"

"Yes grammaw," she offered contritely.

"Mmhm," the woman hummed again through twisted lips. Lil Baby was and would be a lot of things, but contrite would not be one of them. "Anyway, how was school?"

"Fun," Lil Baby admitted. She thoroughly enjoyed being a grown up but being a kid wasn't too bad either. Especially since the little hustler saw plenty of hustles in school. She had spent sixty bucks feeding her crew but didn't mind since she had it. And if ain't trickin if you got it. The hustler in her still preferred to make money rather than spend it.

"What baby?" Big Mama asked when she saw the wheels were turning in the girl's head.

"My friends..." she began but got cut off.

"Your what?" the woman dared and cocked her ear towards her to make sure she could hear the answer. She had made it to sixty and only had one friend, but it took plenty of disappointments and betrayals to understand the lesson she was teaching her granddaughter. Ain't no friends.

"My folks," she corrected and continued. "They smoke weed."

"Mmhm..." Big Mama dared since she didn't drink or use drugs. She viewed drug users as handicaps despite selling them the drugs that crippled them.

"Not me!" she reeled since that lesson was thoroughly drilled into her head after seeing Buella chained to the floor.

"Mmhm," Big Mama hummed once more but believed her. The girl was too smart to repeat the mistakes of her sisters.

"Anyway, they bought some weed from some boy, but it was lil! And all sticks and stems!" she relayed and grimaced to show what she thought of the product. She had seen the fat bags of fluffy, green weed The Family sold in their spots.

"And?" Big Mama asked rhetorically since she already knew.

"I want to sell weed?" she asked and saw the adverse reaction on her grandmother's face. She knew what she said wrong and quickly fixed it. "I mean, have my folks sell it!"

"Well, figure it out first. Then holla back!" Big Mama sighed and picked up her phone. Juice answered within half a ring. "Brang me a couple bags of weed."

A moment later Juice tapped on the door and was summoned inside. He wore a confused look on his face as he handed it over. He paused for an explanation but none was forthcoming. It got even more confusing when Big Mama handed the weed to her granddaughter. A wide smile spread on Lil Baby's face as she stood to head up the street. First, she changed into some after school clothes like she learned from her parents when she had parents.

"You did your homework?" Ethyl asked as she came in as Lil Baby was leaving.

"That's what I'm finna do..." she replied but they were talking about different things. The woman meant the assignments the teachers sent but the girl was thinking about her weed business.

"Now you know them goofy lil hoes up the street can't sell no weed!" Ethyl said once Lil Baby cleared the room.

"They gonna smoke it up, fuck up the money, get tricked out of, get robbed..."

"Mmhm, I know. I know they mamas, so I know all that," Big Mama agreed. "Now she needs to know that and learn how to handle it."

Lil Baby walked down the street with security trailing at a distance. The Hot-Gurls hung out at Jernika's house since her mother was always in the street. That's where the heroin was so that's where she was.

"Come in!" Jernika called to the knock on the door frame. It was just a formality since the door stayed wide open most of the day and night.

"Hey y'all," Lil Baby greeted as she stepped inside.

"Hey gurl. Hey. Sup Lil Baby," came the greetings all around. Meanwhile she looked for a spot to sit down.

"Here you go..." Patty-cake offered and stood.

"Appreciate it, look..." Lil Baby replied and sat. She produced the weed along with her sales pitch. "Instead of buying that garbage y'all bought, with my money, we can sell it!"

"Dang that's pretty!" Jernika cheered and picked it up. "I need to take a picture! Can I get some Wi-Fi?"

"Me too! Me too! I need some..." all the Hot-gurls fussed and pulled their phones. None had money to keep them on so they relied on free Wi-Fi when they could get it. Lil Baby watched as the girls took and posted pictures of the pretty weed. Replies began to pour in almost immediately.

"Ooh! They talmbout, where can they get some!" Patty-cake cheered.

"Tell them brang they money to school tomorrow," Lil Baby replied. "The Hot-gurls got the weed!"

"Uh-oh..." Lil Baby groaned when a police car jumped behind her before she could get off the block. She hadn't traveled far enough to commit any infractions but they lit her up anyway. Lil looked in the mirror as she pulled over and saw her security pullover as well. Now she had to decide if she was going to hop out and make a run for it or not. She wasted too much time debating and soon had cops on each side of the vehicle.

"Do you know why I pulled you over?" one cop asked while the other looked through the windows.

"Uhhh?" she replied since she didn't. She could only hope he didn't ask for license and registration since she had the fake ones Juice brought her along with what was in the bag the second cop was shining his flashlight on.

"You riding dirty?" the first cop asked.

"Got weed in that bag?" the other asked and twisted Lil Baby's lips.

"Tell my grammaw I said I got it. Thank you!" Lil Baby shot back when she realized the lesson in progress. Plus, she remembered the man's face from their daily rounds. She pulled away and had a police escort to school to make sure no real cops pulled her over.

"There she go!" Choo-choo pointed when Lil Baby arrived in the parking lot. She parked and hopped out to get down to business before classes started.

"Ok, these is ten-dollar bags. They cost ten dollars..." Lil Baby explained as she handed off five bags to each of the six girls. She only brought thirty bags since she wouldn't be selling anything herself. Nor would she transport any more after the lesson learned before she even got to school.

"So, I get, fifty bucks?" Jernika asked in disbelief. She had never had more than ten bucks in her hand at one time thus far in life.

"Nah, fifteen. Y'all get three dollars a bag," she replied and waited for the question she knew was coming.

"Why just three bucks?" Patty-cake wanted to know. The yearning in her eyes said she was in search of knowledge.

"Because the weed costs money. That goes back first, we split the change," Lil Baby explained as it had been explained to her. Heads nodded so she continued passing the bags out. As she did, she noticed the boy across the parking lot selling bags of weed himself. Her face scrunched as she tried to place the face, she was sure she had seen before.

"That's that boy Rue. He just started here," Jernika explained. Rue couldn't hear his name being mentioned from across the lot but lifted his head anyway. He and Lil Baby locked eyes as his narrowed into slits. She may not have remembered the incident when they saw each other but he would never forget.

~

"I need more weed!" Jernika announced when the crew met for lunch. She handed over the thirty-five dollars she owed.

"Me too!" Patty-cake and the other girls cheered and cheesed as they paid up. Everyone except Choo-choo.

"Where's your money girl?" Patty-cake demanded just like Big Mama said she would. She didn't name her by name but knew one of the crew would step up and identify themselves as her right-hand man. Just like Ethyl had done in middle school.

"I ain't got it all..." she said and parted with the twenty-three bucks she did have. She only held back the five-dollar bill in her pocket and explained the rest of the short. "Billy finna pay me tomorrow. Short-short get paid Friday. Donna..."

"Bitch you..." Patty-cake began but Lil Baby intervened.

"She's good. Don't even worry about it," she assured and paid for lunch. Big Mama told her not everyone has hustle in them, and you can't get mad when they prove it. Having her in debt was more valuable than the short she took. "The rest of y'all can get some more tomorrow..."

The good weed was in high demand, but the scarcity would make it an even hotter commodity. Plus, she learned not to step on toes unless she wanted a fight. A few other boys sold weed in school, and she didn't want to fight them. No, she had a better plan for them.

~

"Here," Lil Baby demanded as she walked over to the bus stop in the morning.

"What's this?" Choo-choo asked when she shoved the bag into her hands. She explained by nodding at Patty-cake and turning around to head home. Big Mama put her foot down when it came to riding people in the car, she had no business driving anyway.

"You carrying the weed. Since you don't know how to sell it!" Patty-cake explained. "And your ass almost fucked it up for us!"

"I'ma beat her ass 'ifn she do!" Jernika assured. The money in her pocket gave her a sense of pride and she wasn't going to let anyone jeopardize that. The bus hissed to a stop and collected the kids before continuing along its route. High school seniors actually drove most of the school buses, so he knew who they were.

"Let me get one?" he whispered to Patty-cake as she got on.

"I got you..." she explained and took control. She divided up the bags, excluding Choo-choo which gave each girl an extra bag. Each sold a few before the bus pulled into the school. By the time Lil Baby arrived they had sold out. Including the bag Rue bought himself to check out the competition.

"What that shit talmbout?" Rue's right-hand man asked when he returned from copping the bag.

"Check it..." he replied and handed it off while keeping an eye on Lil Baby. She tried to cover her ass with long shirts, but the shape could still be seen. She even tucked her long braids down her shirt so not to offend the girls who permed theirs into oblivion. There was no way to dumb down her pretty, so she made enemies anyway.

"This that gas!" Dallas cheered until the implications caught up a second later. He knew the sticks and stem filled weed they had couldn't compete. "How the fuck we 'posed to compete with this!"

"We not. We finna smoke that," Rue replied as Lil Baby's eyes found him across the parking lot. He nodded as a plan came to mind. Lil Baby cracked a slight smile since she didn't need to read his mind to know what he was thinking.

CHAPTER TWENTY-TWO

"Hey Choo-choo, run and get us some beignets," Lil Baby demanded and passed off a few bills. Choo-choo had secured her position as a gofer when she came short with the money. Which was actually a lot more secure than most other positions.

"Ok!" she reeled and rushed off to fill the lunch time order. The sandwich shop they hit for lunch cost more than the slop served in the lunchroom but tasted better. Quite a few kids ate here instead of there since it was the cool place to be.

"Uh-oh," Patty-cake whispered, wide eyed as an older boy walked in. He looked around as he got into the line, but his face changed when he saw her.

"Fuck you doing in here!" he demanded down at her. His hard face hardened some more when he saw the brisket sandwich on her plate. Mainly because it was the most expensive item on the menu.

"She with me!" Lil Baby shot back loud enough for Vance to take note. "Why you worried about it?"

"He is my brother," Patty-cake explained and cowered under his glaze.

"Long as you ain't with no nigga," he snarled and looked around before getting back in line.

"Awe, he's protective!" Lil Baby smiled. She often wished she had an older brother to protect her and her sisters. But you only get what God gives and make do.

"Tuh!" she huffed and rolled her eyes since having a big brother doesn't always equal protection.

"Look-it..." Jernika said and nodded at the door. Rue and Dallas stepped inside and looked around like they were looking for someone.

"There she go," Dallas announced when he made eye contact with Lil Baby. She shot her eyes over to Vance who was already locked in as the teens approached.

"You Lil Baby?" Rue asked but cocked his head as if it were a dare.

"Err body knows that!" Lil Baby replied sounding more like Bella than herself. She had taken so much from each of her sisters it allowed her to channel from them while still being herself.

"We need to talk bizness?" he asked and looked over her friends to indicate he wanted to talk alone.

"Y'all gimme a sec. Dallas finna buy y'all some dranks..." she replied.

"No, the hell I ain't?" He shot back but Rue understood what he didn't.

"Here. Grab me one too, please," he explained and parted with money he usually wouldn't have spent. The kid had spent too many hungry days and nights to spend money frivolously. Which brought him to his point once they were alone. "Can I re-up with you?"

"Absolutely not," she immediately replied. So fast it took

a second to wipe the pretty smile off his ruggedly handsome face. Lil Baby took note of the dreadlock buds in his hair and clean if older clothes. He was more than his circumstances but had the hustle to achieve success.

"Just like that?" he laughed since he already knew that women need kindness. Some niggas acted like cavemen when it came to chicks but he knew from his history class that the cavemen went extinct.

"I mean, we do the same thing so why would I want competition?" she offered. It was just like the pop quiz she had before lunch but with much more at stake. Much more at steak too since she ate steak and cheese while he was still eating from the lunchroom.

"Well, cuz you ain't going hard. You leaving plenty of bread out chere," he replied since he had done his homework on her even though he wouldn't do it for any of his classes. He was here since the judge gave him the choice of school or juvenile lock up.

"So, err body can eat," she explained just as Big Mama had explained to her. Because the moment she stopped anyone else from eating was the moment she made enemies.

"Check," he nodded since he respected the answer. That didn't solve his dilemma of the weak connect charging him high prices for the mediocre weed. "Thought you might want to expand? Guess I was wrong, sorry to bother you lil lady."

"Baby, it's Lil Baby and it's no bother. I might just want to expand..." she offered coyly along with her number. The lunch bell sounded across the street, so the kids all headed back to class. Choo-choo caught up just in time with the beignets.

"The fuck?" Lil Baby wondered when she saw four football players leading Choo-choo into the locker room. Part of her brain screamed, 'mind yo business' but the other part said, 'she is yo business'. She let out a deep sigh and followed them inside. Her hand fell into her pocket and gripped the straight razor for comfort.

"Me first!" Danford demanded. "Since I am the starting quarterback!"

"That doesn't mean you get to start the train!" his wide receiver shot back. Going first on the train is better than sloppy seconds. And it just gets worse down the line. Poor Choo-choo just looked to and fro amongst the teens. They were all handsome and popular, so she was honored to be selected.

"Un-uh, y'all ain't finna rape my friend!" Lil Baby spat hotly and whipped out the razor when she saw what was going on.

"Rape?" Danford reeled at the ugly word. He was just as mad about the prospect of someone taking some pussy as she was.

"Ain't no body finna rape her!" another of the teens shot back with the same energy as his quarterback. Then explained, "She a hoe. We just finna run a quick train on her is all."

Lil Baby needed a second to process what she was hearing. She still couldn't get with letting one dude inside her let alone four. Her dumb friend sat there dumbfounded and nodding since he was right. She was a hoe and wanted bragging rights of bedding the popular boys.

"Oh, ok," Lil Baby sighed and conceded with one caveat. "Not for free!"

"Huh? What?" they asked and looked between themselves to see if anyone could explain.

"Y'all not finna fuck my friend for free! Give me twenty bucks!" she demanded and stuck out her palm.

"Shit, I got it," Danford sighed and whipped out his wallet.

"Each!" Lil Baby explained while Choo-choo still blinked with a blank mind. She had fucked for free since she started fucking so the concept of getting paid confused her. A fly flying by would confuse her too, so it was a good thing Lil Baby was there. "Twenty bucks each if you tryna fuck!"

"Here! Hmp. Ok," the rest agreed and came out with money. Lil Baby pocketed the cash and rushed away before the football players ravaged her friend.

Danford went first but didn't last very long in the tight, young box. His wide receiver went second and lasted a little longer. The outside tackle had a little more stamina and gave Choo-choo a good pounding. The running back made up the caboose of the train and got off before the bell rang.

"You are a mess!" Danford laughed as he led his crew back out of the locker room. He had to respect it, plus twenty bucks for some pussy is pretty reasonable.

"Whatever, but anytime you wanna fuck her you gotta pay me!" Lil Baby repeated as Choo-choo came out behind them. "Here..."

"For me?" she asked of the forty dollars Lil Baby extended to her.

"Yes! Don't let no one fuck you for free!" she insisted, then added. "Send them to me first."

"Ok," the girl shrugged and became Lil Baby's first whore.

"Here, this for them," Lil Baby explained about the first bag she handed to Patty-cake at the bus stop the following morning. She handed her the other bag and waited for her to ask.

"What's this for?" the girl asked.

"For that boy Rue. He finna give you two hundred dollars. Count it first, then give him this," she explained. She and Rue talked about several topics when he called last night. They finally got down to business and agreed on five bucks a bag. He would be working for her even if he didn't know it.

He scraped up his savings and invested in forty bags of the much better weed. He invested another five bucks in smaller bags in a different color to identify his own brand. He would then stuff the smaller bags to look fatter but still managed to make a few more ten-dollar bags off the same amount. He knew he could get a better price but would play the cards she dealt for now. It was all part of a bigger picture, so he played his position as well.

"Check," she nodded as the bus came hissing and grinding to a stop. The Hot-gurls climbed aboard and headed for the back of the now crowded bus. Kids began migrating on foot to this route so they could cop their weed before the girls sold out.

"Ooh, Look-it!" Choo-choo pointed as they pulled up to the school. All heads turned to see Lil Baby laughing at whatever Rue was saying through the wide smile on her face. They both straightened up when they saw the bus pulling to a stop.

"I'll holla," Lil Baby announced and stepped off so they could handle the transaction. This was a drug deal, so she put some space between her and it.

"You got something for me?" Patty-cake demanded as they approached each other. She took it personally and wouldn't fuck up like Choo-choo had. Not understanding Lil Baby knew the girl would. Even when Choo-choo collected half of what she was owed she kept it for herself. The other half would forever be owed since no one was going to pay her for weed they already smoked.

"Yeah, come on..." Rue said and led the way over to Dallas's car.

Jernika followed behind even though she felt some kind of way about being overlooked to handle the transaction. She had lost her top spot and would probably be making beignet runs soon at this rate. It too was a test, but she didn't know it just yet.

"One ninety-five, six, seven, eight, nine..." Patty-cake counted the mixed bills until they reached two hundred. She passed off the forty bags of weed but didn't budge.

"Um, ok. Thanks," he dismissed and gave Dallas the nod. He hopped in and got down to swapping the weed into the smaller bags. They sold quite a few before the first bell rang. They would sell a lot more before the last bell rang. Then the rest would get sold in their hood.

Rue spent another two hundred dollars the next day and the next for the next couple of weeks. He was flipping his bread like a dope boy should. It wasn't long before he was up a couple of grand. He and Lil Baby agreed on fifteen hundred for a pound, which was quite generous on her behalf.

The Hot-gurls got cuter by the month since they could afford it. New clothes and hairdos upgraded the whole crew. Jernika was still ugly, but the new wig softened the blow somewhat. Rue was making plenty of money himself but didn't spend much of it. He finally decided to make a big purchase to help carry out his big plans.

~

"**S**he hot like fire!" the kid warned as he traded the dirty gun for the cash.

The gun had been stolen from a cop's car by a crackhead who traded it to his dealer in exchange for some crack. The dealer used it against a jacker and put a body on it. It was no more good to him so he sold it for a hundred bucks. It caught another body during a drive-by and got tossed from the window. A heroin junkie found it and sold it to the kid who was now selling it to Rue.

"That's fine, I ain't finna keep it long," he shrugged and came off the agreed upon fifty bucks. Fifty bucks is a lot to a twelve year old so everyone was happy. Even Uncle Calvin who pulled up just as Rue made it home.

"Hey there youngin!" Calvin cheered when he saw the teen again. Rue had grown several inches in the year that passed while he looked just the same. He hadn't heard from him since giving him his number after his grandmother was killed. When he called out of the blue for a ride he happily came.

"Hey dere unc," Rue greeted and hopped into the passenger seat. "What's been up?"

"Just cooling it," he sighed. Calvin took a demotion after Sugar bear got killed since Big Mama wouldn't trust him. Why should she when he derelicted his duty to her and allowed Big Mama to kill the woman. "Finna meet this girl to eat."

"You need some bread?" he asked and reached into his pocket.

"Naw, I got bread. Plus, Lil Baby a rich hoe," Rue replied and watched for a reaction. It took a second before the name furrowed his brow.

"Not Big Mama 'ndem folk?" he wondered since that would be awkward. "That Lil Baby?"

"Mmhm..." Rue said and watched his temples jump as he processed. Rue helped him along and added, "Same one who kilt my grammaw. The one you let kill my grammaw..."

"Boy, what you doing?" Calvin asked and shifted so he could reach the gun under his seat.

"Nuh-uh..." Rue laughed and pulled his first.

"So, what, you a killer now? You finna kill me boy?" Calvin laughed along with him and sped up. He had the drop on him so speeding would prevent him from shooting.

"Yup," Rue replied and fired a round into his temple. The driver's window was painted pink from blood, bone fragments and brain matter. His foot came off the gas pedal when he slumped over, but the car didn't slow until it sideswiped the row of cars parked along the side of the road.

He jumped out when it came to a stop against another car and hopped out. He tossed the filthy gun down to rejoin the vicious cycle of life and death in the city of New Orleans. He finally slowed his pace to catch his breath before arriving for his date with Lil Baby. Not before reciting the rest of his plan out loud. He had been plotting and vowing revenge on the woman who killed his grandmother but had no idea how to get close enough to pull it off.

"Finna kill Calvin, fuck Lil Baby and kill her granny," he said, quite pleased with himself. Now all he had to do was keep doing what he was doing. Getting close enough to Lil Baby to get close enough to put a bullet in Big Mama's head. He didn't care if he lived or died after that since blood debts have to be paid in blood.

. . .

The End

WE RUN
NEW YORK
A ghetto game of thrones

written and directed by
Sa'id Salaam

CHAPTER TWENTY-THREE

1984 Harlem NY

"Ooh that's way too much ass for them Jordache, mami!" Rosalinda squealed as Jennifer turned sideways to admire her ass in the mirror. She had a penchant for being dramatic when it came to complimenting the boss's daughter, but this wasn't that. That really was a lot of ass rounding out those jeans.

"Nah, chica," she said and turned to the other side. She cupped her full breast and let them drop, before puckering her glossy lips. "That's just the right amount of ass!"

"For real tho, them black girls ain't got shit on us Boricuas!" Rosalinda shot back with a mix of pride and racism.

The devil did his job and most of mankind declared its superiority over the rest of mankind just off their race or ethnicity. Which was weird since Puerto Ricans ran the gamut of hues and textures. Like God made a people stew mixed with various shades and textures.

Jennifer's own mother was as white as any Caucasian,

while her dad had a medium brown complexion and could pass for a black man until he opened his mouth. Still, he took more pride in his tiny ancestral island than his new home in New York city. Which was weird too since Puerto Rico is part of America anyway.

Devilish as it may have been, Miguel Camacho's superiority complex propelled him to the top of the food chain in Spanish Harlem. Not an easy feat in an area filled with Columbians, Cubans and Dominicans all vying for the top spot.

He believed that most of life's problems can be solved by throwing money at it. Miguel chunked duffle bags full of cash to the Columbians and became their number one distributor. Now, the Cubans, Dominicans and blacks had to buy from him or go uptown to the Bronx or head out to Brooklyn. Both were extremely dangerous, so they shopped with him. He found that the rest of life's problems can be solved with violence. Miguel had no problem with extreme acts of violence that left a lasting impression on friends and foes alike.

Miguel hoped for a son each time his darling wife Esmeralda got pregnant. Most didn't make it full term until Jennifer came along. He hoped for a prince but had to settle for his princess. The now seventeen-year-old was by far the prettiest in her hood, if not borough.

Jennifer ended up half a hue lighter than her father and inherited the ass his mother's mother inherited from her ancestors in Africa. The heavy breasts were all from Esmeralda's side of the family. The delicate facial features were a mix of both parents. His thick lips, her thin nose, her round chin, his cheek bones. While she adopted her physical traits through genetics the attitude was all her own.

Being the boss's daughter meant she heard him boss a lot of people most of her life. Including her mother who in turn bossed all of her subordinates. As a result, Esmeralda became bossy and told her daughter most of what to do and say. Even who to date since the only dates her overprotective papi permitted was today's date on the calendar. That's why he had a fit when she stepped out of her room to head out for the night.

"No!" Miguel announced in a one-word protest when his daughter came out from her room. The tight T-shirt showed more than he wanted to see so it was a good thing he turned his head before seeing all that ass.

"Tranquillo papi," his wife purred and let her hand slip into his crotch. He may have ruled his hood by force, but she ruled him with sex. Even the promise of sex was enough to get her way most times. This time too since he grumbled to himself and let it go. "Ju look nice mami. Where ju guys going?"

"Just skating," Jennifer lied and kissed her cheek. The skating rink was just uptown, so it was close enough for comfort.

"Have fun," Esmeralda said and pressed a roll of cash into her hand. The woman firmly believed a fat wad of cash was an accessory every woman should carry.

"Thank you mami," she gushed and headed out the door. She had to tuck the cash into her bra since her pants were too tight to use her pockets.

"Follow them Pipo," Miguel ordered as soon as his daughter cleared the apartment.

"On it!" the newest member of his security staff barked and headed out behind him. He was recently promoted after putting in some work on a Dominican crew who set up shop on a block that wasn't theirs to set up shop on. The Camacho funeral home gave them a nice send off.

Jennifer felt like a celebrity when she stepped out onto the block her father ran. Time stopped for a moment while the locals jocked her. The fellas bit their bottom lips at what they would do with that fat ass, while the chicks just admired her Jordache jeans, tight T and bright Reeboks.

"I love summer in New York!" Jennifer cheered as the top came down on her BMW 325.

"Me too!" Rosalinda agreed since she too did love summer in New York. Plus, she was a sidekick and that was her job. She cosigned, agreed, enabled, and facilitated her every whim. Well, most of them since everyone has their own agenda. "Where are we going?"

"Ju will see," Jennifer laughed as she drove past the block that would have taken them to the rink. She turned the knob on the radio so people could sing Ladi dadi along with Slick Rick and Dougie Fresh, booming through her system.

"Where are they going?" Pipo pondered when they missed the turn they should have made. A group of young chicks caught his eye as he drove by so he pulled over to flirt. He would catch up at the rink and stay on her heels all night. Except Jennifer had other plans that didn't include rolling around in circles.

"Where are we going?" Rosalinda asked again when she pulled onto the hundred and fifty ninth street bridge. On one side was Manhattan but the other was another land known as the Boogie down Bronx.

"To see Slick Rick at the Fever!" she cheered and wiggled her ass in the seat.

"Es muy peligroso!" her friend warned, and she was correct. The Bronx was a very dangerous part of a very dangerous city. In truth it was no worse than the hood they just came from. But the danger you know is less dangerous than the danger you don't know.

"My father is Miguel Camacho! I go wherever I want!" Jennifer huffed indignantly at the notion. Like many kids from rich and powerful people she held an air of privilege.

She was partially right though because her father's name rang not just bells but church bells. His organization dropped so many bodies he bought a funeral home. Ironically some of his victims' families paid the debts that got them stretched out through funeral costs. One time one family didn't pay so he had their loved one dumped in front of their building.

"Ju right chica," Rosalinda nodded, but still hit the lock on the locked door to make sure it was locked. As futile as it may have been since the top was dropped. A few turns later they were headed towards the iconic Disco Fever.

"We need some weed!" Jennifer decided and scanned the nearby park for a dealer. Her father's organization sold coke, weed, smack and crack but no one dared sell her a weed seed, let alone a whole bag. Luckily the park near the club contained several dealers, dealing for their daily bread.

"Trey bags! Got that Buddha bless!" a handsome young dealer called Buddha called out to the passersby in the darkened park. His charismatic smile, smooth dark brown skin and incongruent hazel eyes got him sales from women and girls who didn't even smoke weed. Once he put some weight on his wiry six-foot two-inch frame he could be a male model. Not that he would be since he was content with being a pretty thug.

He was from the self-contained world right up the steps on 167th street made famous to the world in The Joker movie years later, but they were always famous in the Bronx. His Highbridge neighborhood did brisk business for his small-time weed operation but the heavy traffic going to the club was good money on a Saturday night.

"Nah yo! We selling these shits as nicks!" Buddha's partnership Rip reminded. His real name was Gabriel Sanchez, but his dark skin and coarse hair made him look more like a Leroy Johnson. The two had been friends since kindergarten and shared the struggle of growing up fatherless in the ghetto. Being fatherless anywhere would be rough, Highbridge made it rougher. As a result, these two eighteen-year-olds were as rough as the concrete jungle that raised them.

"Nicks! Get yo nicks right here!" Buddha switched just as a group of fly girls stomped through on the way to the club. "Sup ladies. Y'all smoking or nah?"

"We good," one shot back with a mouthful of B-girl venom. Only because she kept her eyes straight ahead and hand on her straight razor in her purse. Her friend not only looked but liked what she saw.

"Hole up ma. Let me see what shorty working with," she told her friend and looked Buddha over.

"Nicks of that Buddha bless!" he reiterated and held out a couple of bags in his palm. Weed was sold in tiny manila envelopes back then, so she had to open one to check out the quality.

"Them shits is trey bags on Third Ave!" the first girl huffed as her friend opened the bag.

"Buddha?" she dared once she inhaled the product. She twisted her lips at the brand he put on the regular, brownish weed.

"Tye stick?" Buddha offered along with that smile that was going to get him a lot of pussy in life.

"How bout some regular ass weed!" she shot back and twisted her lips. Lots of people were selling the more exotic chocolate, Lambs bread, Tye stick and Buddha but all these fledgling dealers could get at the moment was regular weed from the Jamaicans downtown. It would still get you high and that's all that matters.

"And they treys!" her friend added. Nonetheless, the girl fished a twenty from her purse and pressed it into his palm. She plucked four of the three-dollar bags from his hand and walked off.

"Son, ma was jocking!" Rip announced as they both watched the wiggling assess wiggle away towards the club.

"Word!" Buddha agreed. Movement from the side stole his attention from the booty show. A well-known stick up kid from University projects was creeping through the darkness. Buddha shifted a little just so he could feel the Saturday night special tucked into his waistband. He felt no fear in general but especially since they grew up together in Highbridge.

"Here come Black Rob," Rip whispered when he picked him up a few seconds later. A few seconds late can easily be a few seconds too late in the streets.

"Sup Black?" Buddha asked since they weren't cool enough to just kick it. If it wasn't business, he could kick rocks as far as he was concerned.

"Let me get a trey?" he asked and tilted his head like people do when they try you up.

"Let me get three bucks!" Rip shot back. He had a twenty-two automatic in his pocket but neither had bust nothing. Yet that is because it was inevitable in this line of work.

"I got y'all after I catch a lick," he said since he was in the darkened park for business as well. The dark and dangerous park saw enough traffic to catch a few licks before heading up the hill to Highbridge.

"Fuck..." Rip began but Buddha cut in before he reached the 'outa here'.

"Word," he said and happily passed off the trey bag. The two friends were equals but Rip accepted the fact that his friend was somewhat smarter than him. After all, Buddha did just graduate from high school, and he never would. Not that he couldn't, he just wasn't interested. He was cool being a hood nigga and you certainly don't need a diploma for that.

"What you do that for?" Rip asked once Black melted back into the darkness like a lion in tall grass. "That nigga ain't never gonna pay up!"

"Son, we just bought a whole nigga for three bucks! Now he can't never ask for shit again," Buddha explained. It made perfect sense but sometimes sense didn't make sense to Rip.

"Fuck that, I want my three bucks!" he grumbled. Three dollars was a lot and could do a lot in those days. Especially for poor kids of poor parents with poor parenting skills. Despite welfare and food stamps they often had to get it from the mud.

Three dollars done right could get a turkey and cheese hero, quart carton of juice, chips, chocolate chip cookies and a loose Newport in any bodega. Some would throw in a free White Owl cigar to roll up the next blunt.

"Word," his friend replied. Not that he agreed, it's just easier sometimes to just say word and be done with it.

"Ok then! Two bad bitches in the rag top Beemer!" Rip announced when the sporty sports car pulled to a stop.

The top raised before they stepped out. Both watched as the two hotties stepped from the car and looked around. They weren't the only cheeba dealers out so the girls had their choice. They looked over Buddha and Rip, then overlooked them in favor of a group of Latino dealers playing salsa music from a boombox.

"Hola mamacita!" one called out as the girls made their way over.

Their bright, gold jewelry seemed to light up the night and that's not good. Once again it was Buddha who spotted the danger a few seconds before his partner. Black Rob eased forward with a black gun at his side. He fell in step so he could kill a few birds with whatever bullets his revolver held. Meaning rob the girls and the dealers at the same time.

"Oh shit..." Rip proclaimed when he finally caught on to his customary a few seconds later. Both knew what was going to happen and had no choice but to let it happen.

The Bronx was affectionately known as the Boogie down but a lesser-known moniker is 'mind your business'. Stick ups were Black Rob's business so they would mind theirs and sell their weed. The robber popped out just as the girls reached the Puerto Rican dealer's bench. He decided to the rob the guys and girls at the same time.

"Run all dat!" Black Rob announced with a sinister chuckle. He was going to spend their cash, smoke their weed and rock their jewels. All that and still not pay Buddha for the trey bag.

"Oh shit!" Buddha laughed when the dealers did the unexpected. They hopped down off the bench and took off running in different directions.

"Wow!" Rip laughed but wouldn't laugh long. One girl began to remove her jewelry but the other put up a protest.

"I am Jennifer Camacho! Miguel Camacho's daughter! I'm not giving you shit!" Jennifer protested and took a swing at him with her Gucci bag. Buddha cracked a smile since she had heart, but Black Rob cracked her jaw.

"Oh shit!" he exclaimed when the robber dropped the girl with a right hook. He spun and knocked the other one down as well.

"Come off all this shit!" he growled and began snatching the chains from their necks. Rosalinda put up no resistance, but Jennifer was cut from the same rugged cloth as her father. She put up a fight for hers until Black Rob socked her again in her eye.

"Ju got that," Jennifer nodded. One eye was closed but she mentally took pictures of the man with the other so she could describe him in vivid detail to her father. Black Rob took it a step further and fondled her breast. He looked around and made a life-changing decision.

"Take them pants off!" he demanded. He could definitely sell the expensive jeans but was after something far more valuable. He had no idea the girl was a virgin but planned to rape her anyway. "Bout to fuck the shit out yo fine ass bitch!"

"Fuck you going?" Rip asked when Buddha took off in their direction. There was no time to explain to him, so Buddha just explained to the would-be rapist.

"Yo son, you bugging!" he announced when he reached the robber. Jennifer focused her one eye on him to take his picture too. He was dying too just for being out here. She would have the attendant at the gas station murdered too for not washing her windows. The Camacho funeral home was about to get real busy over tonight's happenings. Some people are just not to be fucked with. Jennifer Camacho was some people.

"Say what?" Black Rob asked with his face straining to understand why he was in his business. Even Rip couldn't figure it out and they were best friends for life.

"Bruh, you got their bread and jewels. Take the money and

202

run," he suggested while the man still struggled to get her pants off.

"Tell you what..." Black Rob growled and began to turn his gun in that direction. He was a known shooter, so Buddha didn't wait to get shot. He whipped out his own gun before he saw the black hole that could put a hole in him. Flight or fight kicked in and his body went into autopilot. He watched as the gun bucked and sent a slug right into Black Rob's right eye.

"Yooooo!" Rip shouted when the same slug came out the back of his head. He may have been stuck but Buddha remained calm.

"Y'all get up! Get out of here!" he told the fallen girls. He reached for Jennifer's hand to help her up, but she initially pulled away.

The girl was so shaken by nearly being raped. She looked over and the mangled mess that was once a stick-up kid and snapped out of it. She accepted the helping hand and climbed to her feet. Rosalinda was on her own since Rip wasn't as chivalrous as his friend.

"Puto!" Jennifer growled and kicked Black Rob in his head. She slipped in the puddle of blood and went back down.

"We must be waiting for five-o?" Rip wondered since they were still at a murder scene. It was a justifiable homicide, but they weren't planning on waiting around for the cops to come.

"Let's bounce!" Buddha agreed and turned to leave once he helped Jennifer back to her feet.

"Don't leave us! I can't fucking see!" Jennifer shouted since her eye was completely swollen shut from the blow. More like demanded like a diva, used to demanding people.

"Have your girl push the whip!" Rip shouted since he was ready to run up those tall ass stairs and go home.

"I can't drive!" Rosalinda moaned. Like quite a few New

Yorkers spoiled off trains, buses, ferries, taxis, and gypsy cabs, never would learn to drive.

"Fuck!" Buddha shouted and conceded. He took the outstretched keys and pulled Jennifer along to her car. A few minutes later they crossed back over to Manhattan. A few minutes later they reached their block. That's when all hell broke out.

www.ingramcontent.com/pod-product-compliance
Lightning Source LLC
Chambersburg PA
CBHW051951220626
47052CB00004B/905